Kirstie's Witnesses

Kirstie's Witnesses

Sheenagh Pugh

Published by The Shetland Times Ltd.,
Lerwick, Shetland.
1998

Kirstie's Witnesses

ISBN 1 898852 39 1
First published by The Shetland Times Ltd., 1998.

Cover illustration by Alexa Rutherford.

British Library Cataloguing-in-Publication Data
A catalogue record for this book is available from the British Library.

Printed and published by
The Shetland Times Ltd.,
Prince Alfred Street,
Lerwick, Shetland, ZE1 0EP, UK.

Foreword

Christina Inkster Jamieson, a.k.a. Kirstie Caddel, was a real person, as is every other named character in this book; even the women chatting at the well can be found in the annals of the Lerwick Parochial Board. But since I wanted to write a novel rather than an historical account, the personalities, conversation and motivation I have ascribed to them are obviously my responsibility rather than theirs.

The real Kirstie's story is contained in several documents, notably the minutes of the Parochial Board, an application form, and evidence given at a trial and an inquiry. These documents are all in the Shetland Archive and I was able to study them there because of the generous co-operation of Brian Smith, Chief Archivist of Shetland, without whose help I could have got nowhere. It was an article by Mr Smith in Vol. VIII of the *Shetland Folk Book* which first made me want to write this book.

I should also thank Mr Smith and Mr John J. Graham for kindly reading the manuscript and advising on points of history and dialect; Mrs Margaret Stuart Robertson, who kindly let me see material on the Duncan family from her then forthcoming book *Sons and Daughters of Shetland 1800-1900* (published by The Shetland Publishing Company, 1991); Dannie Abse, who enlightened me on some aspects of Dr Cowie's post-mortem report, and Robin Reeves, for his help while I was preparing the manuscript. I am also grateful to the Welsh Arts Council for financial assistance.

The dialect Kirstie and her friends spoke would have been further removed from standard Scottish English than I have rendered it: I have tried to show the difference between her spoken idiom and the written language of educated people of the day, without making her sound too alien, for she should not strike anyone in modern Britain as a stranger.

Sheenagh Pugh.

PART ONE

NORTHMAVINE

Chapter 1
1824: Summer

On the foreshore of the voe, a great many shellfish washed up. Among the shingle, the sun would pick out the pearl of empty scallops, the blue iridescent mussels, and the pink husks of crabs. Sometimes the stones themselves glittered, with quartz or mica. There was no sand at that point, but further down the voe, where it opened out, was a little islet joined to the mainland by an ayre, a thin curved strip of sand that glinted white. And beyond that, beyond all land, the great northern ocean was a sheet of light, so bright the eye could not rest on it.

Under heavy cloud, you would have called all this grey. Often the mist would lie low enough to blank out the reddish cliffs that rose on the far side of the voe, and the fields that sloped more gently down to the foreshore on the near side. When there was nothing to reflect but an iron sky, the place looked everything that was depressing, and it could look like that for a long time. It was the grey of a uniform, a tombstone.

But there were days when the mist scrolled back into a sky of the clearest, most remote blue. On days like that, the shingle was metallic, the water glassy; the whole landscape seemed one vast reflecting surface. Those days, you lived in light.

There was a child, about ten or eleven, working her way along the foreshore, stooping now and then. She was meant to be collecting live shellfish for food. Her basket was fairly full now, though, and being a child she was turning her mind to other matters. Things with hinges, like empty mussels and crab claws, make satisfying noises and movements; flat stones skim across the water leaving rings of light. She went barefoot, feeling with her toes the smooth coolness of rock, the crunch of powdered shells and the slippery, greasy wetness of seaweed. Had it been winter, she might have been collecting the seaweed; it was stored for manuring the fields in spring. Some of it was edible, too, and when their pasture was under snow the sheep would come down to the voe's edge and feed on it, looking mildly puzzled when a salty wave broke around their feet.

Eventually she turned her back to the voe and scrambled up the bank to the fields above the shore. In the bank's crevices, sea-pink grew wherever it could get a hold, but it was out of flower now, the small heads on their stalks colourless above the tuft of grassy leaves. In their season, if you looked down from the hills, the pink flowers formed a haze, inches above the ground. Now was the turn of the tormentil, which grew on the higher land where the sheep grazed. It was too short for them to crop: four yellow petals flat to the ground, and it gave the hill a glow, like a buttercup held up to the chin.

"Kirstan! Kirstan!". The voice sounded flustered and impatient; the child hastened her steps toward a small grey clump of buildings around a cottage that faced the sea. Outside it, a woman was prodding the last of the cattle into the byre for milking. At the same time she tried to comfort a little girl of about eight, who was clinging to her dress and crying, having slipped and fallen in the sea of muck outside the byre.

"Kirstie, wash da peerie[1] ting, I canna leave da coo. An put da shells ida pot. Whit is du gotten?"

"Spoots", said Kirstie, showing the basket of razorshells. But the woman's attention was already back with the cattle. Kirstie took the crying child's hand and led her to the house. Going in was like putting the light out. There were no windows: what light there was came from a skylight in the roof, but it had to filter through the canopy of peat smoke that settled about the rafters. On a rope, stretched across the room, there hung a flickering fish-oil lamp. Kirstie moved it along the rope to where a wooden water bucket stood near the door, and started to wash the child, singing a naming-song for parts of the body to make a game of it. After a few moments, the child stopped crying and joined in.

When they went out again to look for their mother, there had been a change in the weather: a sharp shower of rain out of a sky suddenly grey. There were some clothes drying outside; the two girls had to hurry to get them into the house. By the time they were put away, the rain was over. The little one exclaimed with delight at the rainbow against the diminishing greyness.

Kirstie nodded and pointed away down towards the voe. On the water lay the perfect, sharp-edged reflection of the rainbow.

1 "peerie": little.

4

Chapter 2
1824: Winter

Fleein far but fedderless,
New come oot o Paradise,
Fleein ower sea an laund,
Deein in me haund.

The old man leaned back and enjoyed the concentration in the child's face as she tried to puzzle it out. She knew most of the old riddles by now: it was rarely he remembered one she hadn't heard. She frowned, raising her eyes from the sock she was knitting, and looked intently round; the answer was often some household object. The smoke curling from the peat fire in the middle of the room ... it could be said to fly far, even to die in someone's hand, but it hardly came from Paradise. No article of furniture, like the stools or her mother's chair, did any of those things. Nor the iron pots, nor the wooden water buckets, nor the bannocks her mother was shaping at the table on the other side of the hearth. She glanced up to the rafters, partly boarded over to form a loft space where salt fish and meat were curing in the swirling peat smoke. And higher up again, to the skylight in the roof where the smoke finally slipped out into a leaden winter sky. Flying far ... but featherless, so not a bird. Outside the thick stone wall, the wind kept up a low, steady sound like a single note of music. Flying over sea and land ... the wind did that, indeed, but it didn't die in your hand; it slammed into you. She shook her head: her eyes returned, comically baffled, to the old man's face.

Smiling, he got stiffly off the big wooden chest they were sitting on and went across, past the hearth, to the house door. As he took it off the latch, a terrific blast of icy wind blew in: the child cried out softly with the sudden cold, and her mother exclaimed in sharp protest.

He had to take both hands to the door to close it again. But then he bent to the floor and scooped up something which had come in with the wind. He held it out to the child: a handful of snow crystals, already melting on his palm. More than her former puzzlement, he enjoyed the smile that slowly spread as she matched the riddle's lines, one by one, with their object.

The woman at the table glanced over her shoulder at them, without pausing in her work. Her hands performed functions like knitting, washing, baking, automatically, no longer needing either her eyes or her will to inform them. Rather, it was their natural condition to be doing something: it was being at rest that would have come hard to them.

"Whit for is du lettin da caald ida hoose? Better if du'd mend da nets for Robert, den blether. An Kirstie, dunna sit wi haunds idle, finish dy sock." She did not sound angry or complaining: the voice with its constant exhortations toward the next job was as automatic as the working hands. It was like the one note of the wind. The old man grinned sheepishly at the child, as if they were fellow□conspirators caught in mischief; then he went to the corner where a tangle of fishing nets lay, brought them back over to his chest and began to sort through them. His wife finished with the bannocks, took up a bucket and disappeared through the connecting door that led to barn and byre, built on to the house for warmth. As the door closed, the old man began to sing softly:

Farewell Parker. thou bright angel,
Once thou was the navy's pride.
Though they hanged him up for mutiny ....

His voice trailed off; his blue eyes were filmed over, as if the words or some other thing eluded him.

Hercules Inkster was a seaman. For that matter, so was nearly every crofter in Shetland. Fishing for the laird was a condition of tenancy, it was how you paid the rent. Each May, the little townships became a country of women, children and greybeards, when all the men who were fit to take an oar went to the deep-sea fishing ground, the haaf. Out there, you spent days and nights at sea, maybe with a break midweek when you took the fish back to the nearest beach to dry, and slept on a wooden bench in a hut. Then you went to sea again until Saturday, and home for the weekend. This went on until August, generally with some loss of life along the way. Then the laird's merchant calculated the value of the fish you had landed, offset it against the goods he'd supplied you, and worked out that you were still in debt. It was how things were done.

Some young men, who despaired of ever getting rich this way, tried the Greenland whaling. But Hercules, though he began as a fisherman, had done a lot of his sailing on board Royal Navy ships, fighting Napoleon. It was because of his long absences during the wars that he was fifty-two when the child sitting beside him was born.

She came as a total surprise to him, when he tramped home after his final discharge; his wife had no means of sending him word that his brief leave, three years before, had produced this consequence. His other children were nearly grown, even the youngest was thirteen, and he had been absent from so much of their lives that there seemed now to be no space for him. The little one, toddling about in the way with nothing particular to do, struck a chord in him: he took to having her with him when he worked the fields, or went to fetch peats from the hills. He felt more like her grandfather than her father. Even the birth of another daughter, the year after he came home, did not much impinge on this relationship. By the time young Mary was running about the place, Kirstie was already the one who followed him about; who learned songs and riddles from him and was always ready to listen to his war stories.

She glanced up at him again, though this time she didn't stop knitting. "Tell me aboot da trees." That was a funny thing about children, they never got tired of hearing the same story, which made them good companions for old men who never tired of telling it. And you could never guess what would take their fancy. He had told Kirstie any number of exciting, and not always strictly accurate, tales of battles and dangers: even sea-monsters had made the odd appearance, but the only miracle that amazed her was the true one: the great living monsters, like a briar or a rose, but with stems as thick as a man's body, towering above a house and ending in a roof of green that shut out the sky. Apart from a couple of stunted elders by the church, grown as a windbreak, she had never seen one.

"Aye ... I mind da trees o' Funchal, in simmer, full o' birds nestin. Ye cudna see da birds for da green laeves, an it wis like da trees were singin by demsells. Yon birds didna skirl an skreech laek wir bonxies an maas². Fifes an fiddles cudna mak a bonnier tune, an a' alang da road da green trees sang." The connecting door opened, and he hurriedly busied himself about the nets again, but it was only little Mary.

"Kirstie, Mammy says to tak da kale to da lambs." Most of the sheep fended for themselves in the cold, but each year's lambs would winter in the lamb house. Kirstie slipped down from Hercules' sea-chest and went over to the table where her mother had left the knife and the head of kale. In a surprisingly short time she had it chopped small and was off to the barn. Mary followed, to find out which job came next.

Left alone, the old man let the nets fall again. In truth, there was no special hurry for them; nobody was going to need them until May. It was just that his wife felt acutely uncomfortable at the sight of someone not working. He could understand why. Her own tasks, the cooking and cleaning and suchlike, went on all year, but there was a limit to what a man could do around a croft in winter. There could be little outdoor work done, and if any did arise, there was his tall son; the one who had been fifteen when Hercules came home for good and who had

2 "bonxies and maas" : skuas and gulls

looked at him warily, the man of the house sizing up an intruder. Now that Hercules had given up going to the haaf fishing in summer, he was disturbed to realise how much happier he was during the weeks when Robert was away, and he could feel of some use. Although, God knew, Margaret had managed well enough without him for years, and could again. Aboard ship, he had thought constantly of coming home; now he felt someone had moved it while he was away. He thought often of the crew of HMS *Hero*, of which he had been a part: its rigid hierarchy, its certainties, its deep ties of mutual need. That crew was all gone now, and *Hero* too, lost on the Haak Sands on 25th December, when newfangled folk celebrated Christmas Day[3].

In the byre, Kirstie drew a deep breath, clutched her basket of kale close, and ran out into the swirling, snow- laden wind. The lamb house was just across the yard, fortunately: an upturned boat resting on low stone walls. She ducked inside and scattered the kale in the stuffy darkness, scented with hay and dung and warm bodies. One of the young sheep nuzzled her; it had been orphaned and brought up in the house and now found its own kind alien and frightening. She stayed with it a while, listening to its occasional bleats, the snuffling and munching of the others, the hooting of the wind outside, and trying to picture the long road of singing trees.

3 "Christmas Day" : At this time, and for long after, Shetland still used the old Julian calendar, so that Christmas was celebrated on 5th January and New Year's Day on 12th January.

Chapter 3
1825: Christmas

Kirstie and Mary lay in the dark warm tent of the bedcovers. Mary was still asleep, but Kirstie was listening to the small sounds in the next room. Someone moving quietly on the earth floor. A sputter in the peats as they came to life after resting under ash overnight. And another sound, not an everyday one, a soft hiss repeated over and over. Then the moving person opened the door and his footfalls diminished toward the byre.

She inched her head outside the covers, trying not to let too much cold air in. The fire hadn't had a chance to warm the house yet; besides, it was earlier than their normal waking time. She peered across to the bed on the far wall of the room, trying to see in the dark whether her mother was awake. There was no sound or movement from her, but she might just be keeping quiet, prolonging the moments of peace before any demands were made of her. In the bed above herself and Mary, Kirstie could hear a soft rhythmic snore which meant Robert was still asleep. That wasn't surprising: she knew he and her father must have been up late last night with the neighbours, for they had come home laughing and shushing each other long after she was in bed. But Hercules was up early; would never fail to be up early this one day of the year.

She had moved the covers further than she intended: Mary stirred and muttered in a half-sleep. Kirstie nudged her, but instead of waking she cuddled closer. Kirstie smiled. She had never slept alone. In a croft, you slept with your parents while you were a baby; when you got old enough, or the next baby came along, you went to join your brothers or sisters, as the case might be. Kirstie had gone from her mother to Anne, who was eleven when she was born, and a few years later Mary had joined them. Anne had never slept alone either: she too had joined a much older sister, now long grown up and gone. Robert, being the only boy, had been alone since he left his mother's bed, which was maybe why he was so quiet and self-sufficient. Kirstie couldn't imagine how he could sleep, without the convivial whispering that warmed his sisters' nights. She missed Anne, married the year before.

She could hear the footsteps returning from the byre, and nudged

Mary again, more urgently. The little one protested sleepily: "It's no' mornin' yet."

"It is: it's Yule mornin'. Daddy's bringin' da licht."

They both sat up, holding the covers round them. The dark was less now, indeed an unusual amount of light was flooding through the gap between the ben end, where the beds were, and the but end, or living space. It was Hercules' and Margaret's box bed that formed the partition between the two rooms, and looking across, they could see their mother more clearly now: she was awake, and nodded to them.

In the gap of light at the bed's end, a tall, stooped figure appeared. He looked dark at first, for not only did he stand in light, he carried it high in front of him, as a priest might. The light came from a candle, not in a normal holder of any kind but balanced in a network of white gleaming bones: it was a cow's skull, with the candle fixed in the eye socket. Kirstie knew which cow's head it came from; her mother had made broth of it three days earlier. She wondered if the other cows had recognised it, when her father fed them by the candle's light that morning.

In his other hand, the priestly figure held a cup. He went over to Margaret's bed and held it to her lips. She sipped, making a slight grimace: it was whisky and fairly raw spirit at that, but it was the custom. Then he crossed the room and reached up to his son. The light had stirred Robert awake by now, and to judge by his sigh of relief as he drank, he found the whisky therapeutic. Then it was Kirstie's and Mary's turn.

Kirstie sipped with the same dislike as her mother. It was not a taste likely to please children, but she had other reasons too. Families like the Inksters did not use spirits often, not having the means, but there were festivals, especially around Yule, and it was not hard for a child to notice the difference in the behaviour of adults who unaccountably liked the fiery, disagreeable stuff. She did not care to see how it led steady, sensible Robert on to make a giggling fool of himself; still less to see Hercules growing quieter and more dangerous while Margaret watched her words with uncharacteristic care.

The man with the light moved back to the but end, his family following. This was the part of the ritual Kirstie and Mary liked best. The living space blazed with light, not the smoky flicker of the kollie lamp but the clear, steady flame of candles; new ones and old ends saved up for months. They ate breakfast in this light. Hercules set the cow's skull in the middle of the table and Margaret brought out the Yule brunnies, round oatcakes with their rims pinched into a pattern like the sun's rays. It was like an act of defiance, this festival. To spend candle; to be prodigal of light in the midst of the dark time; to eat the very sun. You could say it made no difference, for the spendthrift light was soon snuffed, while outside it was still dark most hours of the twenty-four, and would be for many weeks yet. But it burned itself into the memory, a promise that winter could not last for ever.

It was a strange day altogether, for no work but the strictly necessary could be done. What there was fell as a matter of course to Margaret, but even she spent much of the day in uneasy idleness, her fingers twisting from time to time in and out of non-existent knitting. Hercules and Robert were off playing a game of football which involved all the men of the district and minimal rules. It went on as long as daylight lasted: Kirstie and Mary watched it, on and off, wandering away periodically to play their own games, visit the ex-pet in the lamb house, or go back to their mother for more of the food which was in such unusual plenty for this one day. It was like a day out of the calendar, when time came to a stop and no rules applied.

Later, when dark came on, company gathered in the house. Most nights of Yule, there was dancing and music in someone's place. The young folk would dance in the barn, coming together from all over the district and maybe taking the chance to court someone they normally only saw in church. Winter was a time of relative leisure, a good time for meetings and understandings. Last year, Anne and her young fellow had been wrapped up in each other around this time, kissing in what they imagined were private moments while Kirstie and Mary spied round barn doors and giggled. This year, Kirstie watched the couples with less mockery, wondering if there might not be something in it, though she didn't admit as much to Mary.

A little out of the circle of the dancers, they bounced and twirled on their own to the fiddle music. It was impossible not to move to it. The fiddler grinned as he looked around: children who didn't know the steps yet, old men whose shuffling feet knew them by heart; they might all have been on the end of his strings. When he paused, they could sense their tiredness; some leaned against the wall laughing and gasping, but he knew that the minute he struck up again, their aching feet would find more spring from somewhere. He felt he could make them dance all night long, maybe to death or to another world like the trow[4] fiddlers of legend. Deciding they'd had long enough, he struck a new tune: the reel *Lasses Trust In Providence*.

Kirstie studied a group of young boys about her own age, already bored with the dance and stifling laughter as they plotted some mischief. She wondered if she would fall in love with any of them when they were older; it seemed hardly possible. Yet it would not be long now before they went to the haaf in summer with their fathers: they would grow into men who were forever going away, and coming back again if they were lucky, while she would grow into a woman like her mother,

4 "trow" : troll

who seemed to have spent half her life waiting for a man to come back from somewhere. There were women like that all over the district, with a son or brother or husband in the Navy, or the merchant service, or the Greenland fishery, or just the haaf, which might be closer but could be as dangerous as any of them. If it came to that, a man could drown in the voe, within sight of his own house, if the sea felt like it.

Robert spun by in the dance, and ruffled her hair as he passed; he had a kindness for his little sisters. Though he was twenty-four, he was not courting any girl yet. He was very close to their mother, she having leaned on him so much in Hercules' absence, and he being, too, her only son. They were an alliance: Kirstie never saw them together, earnestly discussing the crops or the rent, without feeling excluded.

Kirstie and Mary wandered back to the house while the dancing was still going on. It might last till the early morning; those who lived at a distance would sleep on straw in the barn. Back at the house, some older folk were chatting sleepily, while Margaret eyed some clothes she wanted to wash and Hercules played the fiddle softly in the background. He wasn't as good as the man in the barn, but he had the old tunes. He had played them to his shipmates, but had not been there to pass them on to his son, so the skill would die out of the family with him.

The cow's skull lay in a corner, no different now from any of the everyday webs of bone you could see bleaching in the pasture; the delicate, tiny skulls of birds, the long, surprisingly elegant ones of sheep, the ungainly hulks of cattle. The end of candle had been carefully removed from the eye-socket, to be saved for another day. It was just a dead thing now, and the tall priest, the bringer of light, just an old man wondering if the audience would stand for another story about the Bay of Biscay.

But one of Kirstie's earliest memories was of the old man bringing the light, in its polished white sconce of death, against the darkness. When she was smaller she had once asked him, in the middle of a long winter, to bring the sun back, and had been amazed to learn that there was anything he could not do.

Chapter 4
1836

On the beach, nearly all the women, children and old men of the township were assembled. Some were eating, a bannock or some tatties hastily grabbed before they left their dinner on the table. Most had brought sharp implements of some kind: peat spades, knives, scythes; and the children made a great play of stabbing these into the sand. The old men sat down, lowering themselves to the shingle with plentiful complaints about their rheumatism. But most of the women stayed upright, craning to see the dark shadows at the mouth of the voe. A semicircle of boats was moving in, looking tiny at that distance, and there carried faintly on the air the sound of shouting, and the blowing of horns. From a little headland further down the voe, a boy came running back toward the beach.

"How many?" a middle-aged woman called to him. Though she looked old enough to be a grandmother, she had a small baby in her shawl, eyes tight shut, nuzzling like a seal pup. The boy shouted back: "Maybe forty." Her eyes shone; she breathed deeply with lips parted.

In front of the boats, the shadows advanced hesitantly, as if they disliked the course they were taking but could see no other. Just at the voe's mouth, some did turn aside. At once, two of the boats veered out of the semicircle, and the watchers on the beach saw the ocean's face shatter with light as stone after stone was hurled to direct them back.

The old men explained to each other how much better they would have managed the boats themselves. Most of the women were either calculating the current price of thirty or forty barrels of whale oil, or had eyes and thoughts only for the boats: one of those shadows turning and lashing out could smash a boat easily. Disregarded, and sensing the adults preoccupied with other things, the children had wandered down to the voe's edge, to skim stones or play with sticks, amusing themselves by stirring up little swirls of mud and sand in the water's fantastic clarity. An infant, tongue stuck out in concentration, arranged shells and seaweed in a complicated, private pattern. Once he reached into the water to collect something he fancied, and cried out with the unexpected cold.

The dark shapes were coming on down the voe, the boats after them. The men in the boats were making all the racket they could, especially with the shrill horns, and it seemed as if the pursued wanted above all else to escape the noise. They did not come willingly, like some tame beast to an unsuspected slaughterhouse; they were hesitant and wary, knowing this was not the way to safety. But between them and the open sea were the horns and shouts, and the vibration of stones through the water: it seemed a wall of pure sound could hold their powerful bodies back.

The watchers on the beach held their breath, knowing that even now, if just one turned and smashed its way through the wall, the others would follow: it could happen. If it did, the fishing boats would be little protection. The keener-eyed could make out individuals in the boats now. Margaret Inkster, whose eyes were still sharp enough at close range but saw little further than her knitting, was asking fretfully: "Whaur's Robert?".

"Robert's fine, Mammy", answered Kirstie, not turning her eyes from the water. She was watching Robert's boat, but not Robert. Beside her, Mary stifled a laugh and whispered: "Du's no' seein' Robert, no' whin James is ida boat forbye". Kirstie grinned and pushed her shoulder.

As the shapes came closer, the old men got painfully to their feet. The mothers began to shush the children and call them away from the edge. It was important for the beach to be silent, a refuge from the noise of the boats. They all shifted higher up, forming a semicircle around the beach that mirrored the pattern of the boats in the voe. And there was total quiet, except that the baby in the shawl raised a thin wail. His mother reached under the shawl and latched him on to her breast. Even the sounds of sucking seemed loud.

The boats had their quarry ringed in now; there was nowhere else for them to go. The men had quietened down, taking a breather. As the huge bodies drifted into the shallows, the glassy water clouded with mud. The first one beached on the shingle: a full-grown pilot whale, twenty feet of glistening blackness. In the immensity of ocean, moving in his own element, he would have looked slender and graceful: stranded on the foreshore among the little people he was monstrous, ungainly. His flippers, surprisingly slim and pointed, had no chance of moving or directing his vast bulk; he settled it down on the shingle with an incongruous little sigh.

Men were jumping from the boats, wading through the shallows to the whales. Two were at the leader now, one lifting up a fin while the other drove his harpoon in, aiming at the heart. Nothing happened at first; there was a long moment of perfect stillness, as if the whale had died instantly. Then a sudden terrific convulsion arched his whole body,

14

and the men leaped clear as the thrashing tail drenched the beach with mud and water. They ran on then, to the next. More had beached; the smaller ones, not quite stranded, were being dragged up the shore, a man at either fin. Some of these were young ones, and the mothers came after them at all hazard, not caring what was in their way. But most of the whales still in the water seemed to be queuing up, waiting their turn. Around their rolling, glistening bodies, the water was changing colour again; through the cloudy, yellowish-brown a deep crimson welled up and spread slowly outward across the voe.

The whales which had been struck took a long time to die, jerking and convulsing for many minutes after the men had moved on. Sometimes women and children would widen the wounds, or make new ones. The woman with the baby in her shawl seemed particularly active at this, stabbing again and again, rhythmically, until she was exhausted.

Hercules Inkster watched her for a moment, then looked away across the blood-red water; years away. Kirstie touched his arm and he turned and walked off toward his croft. When he moved, it was seen how the sea cold had settled in his bones and stooped his tall figure.

Later, shifting restlessly on his sea-chest, he watched Kirstie heating water at the fire for Robert and the young man her eyes had followed in the boat, James Jamieson from Olnafirth. Kirstie's James. He and Robert glowed in the firelight, their arms red to the elbows. Robert, thirty-six now and looking maybe ten years older, was excited, for him.

"Forty, say twa, tree pound apiece; it cud be a hundred, or better ..."

"Aye", said James, drily, "an' after the laird taks da third o' it, for the 'damage ta his foreshore' ? And wha will we sell the oil tae, but his merchant, and wha fixes the price, but da pair o' dem?"

"Well, dat's da wye o' it an' always was." Robert eyed James uneasily, as if he had suggested an alteration in the path of the planets.

"No' everywhaur. Da Lerook[5] fishermen sell whaur dey laek. An' get paid in cash, no' in goods yon merchant sets his ain price on"

"Whit's da guid o' cash? We'd still need ta change it for meal an' nails an' shoes."

"Aye, but we'd no' need ta sell cheap an' buy dear! If da laird lets only one merchant at the place, he buys an' sells as he laeks. But Lerook's a street o' merchants, an' if ane maks hard bargains, folk can try anidder."

Most conversations between Robert and James turned into this argument. Kirstie always listened keenly, because it was clear that she was going to marry James; officially they were planning to rent a croft in Olnafirth, but whenever James talked about Lerwick she could hear a different note in his voice, an enthusiasm which nothing else kindled

5 "Lerook" : Lerwick.

there and which she had never heard from anyone else. Robert was shaking his head, certain that things must be as they had always been; that they would just clear the rent in a good year and fall behind in a bad one, and die in debt to the laird and his merchant like everyone else.

When one man owned near enough all the land in the district, and could tell you where to do all your buying and selling, what happened to people like Robert was easy to understand. They were hard-working, but desperately apathetic; they weren't interested in trying any improved method of doing a thing, because they saw no profit to them in it, and they were convinced that nothing they did could make a difference. It was their passivity, which visitors sometimes called peaceableness, that had made them such a prize for the press-gangs during the war; the Navy loved them not only for their seamanship but because they had a positive aptitude for doing what they were told.

Kirstie was basically as peaceable as any of them. She could understand why Robert became so uneasy when the familiar order of things was questioned, and half-shared his fatalism. But it interested her that James thought things could be different. Over the last couple of years, Hercules had given gradually in. He had surrendered to the ache in his bones, and hardly stirred beyond the yard. He had given up all hope of getting the better of his debts: Kirstie knew he owed the merchant more even than most of their neighbours did, and had stopped worrying about it. Indeed, he let Margaret and Robert do all the worrying; he had accepted them as an alliance and retired to the margin of his own family. He was only seventy-five or so, which by Shetland standards was not all that old. When Kirstie was a child, and he in his late fifties, he had seemed unimaginably old to her, but always vigorous, active and handy. Now she saw him from an adult's eye, no longer impossibly, Biblically ancient and yet older in every way that mattered. It was a long time since she had thought there was nothing he could not do.

She studied him as he sat hunched on the chest, trying to warm the pain out of his twisted hands. In his longsighted, seaman's eyes the light had gone milky. And in Robert's patient face, the pale copy of his father's, no light had ever kindled. But James, walking up and down and still arguing, caught the glow of the fire. His face was like any other young fisherman's, except for the energy and fervour which animated the features and turned plainness into something else. He looked as if he still believed he could do whatever he set out to; as if he could make things happen, rather than wait for them to happen to him. He was still talking about Lerwick: Kirstie tried without success to imagine a whole street of shops. It sounded no less implausible than Hercules' avenue of singing trees.

16

Down at the foreshore, the blue half-dark of summer had come, but though many of the crofters had gone home, some were still flensing the blubber from the carcasses. On the whaling ships, there were contrivances for that, which spiralled the whale round and round and took the blubber off in a long strip: here it was a case of hacking it away with peat spades. The carcasses were left to lie; it was the oil people valued, not the meat. Already there was a riot of shouting, exuberant seagulls about the beach, but it would be weeks before the huge, arching ribs were picked clean.

The little boy who had been arranging shells and seaweed wandered disconsolately between the skinned hulks, looking for his vanished pattern. Now and then, he set his shoulder to one of them and heaved, as if he hoped it might still be underneath.

For as far as could be seen out in the voe, the water was crimson; so deep a red that one glanced up automatically at the pale sky, looking for the sunset that was not there.

PART TWO

LAND OF OPULENCE

Chapter 5
Lerwick: Summer, 1839

I certainly expected to find Shetland far before Faroe but I did not imagine that the inhabitants of the first named islands would be in possession of all the comforts and luxuries which we read of in books as so abundant in England. The neat houses. the handsome apartments. the floors all carpeted, the elegant grates ornamented with bright polished brass. Everything made me feel that I had come to the land of opulence.
             - Christian Ployen, Governor of the Faroes.

Christian Ployen gazed out from Hay and Ogilvy's office window over Freefield dock, and wondered how many barrels the fishing industry could need. Below him, every cooper in creation seemed to be at work, the contrasting notes of their hammers on wood and metal merging into something that was almost music. Mingled in with it were the shouted directions from the dockers unloading a vessel, and snatches of song, which he suspected were bawdy, from a group of girls gutting fish. They had coarse, weather-tanned faces and a free-and-easy manner with men, from working so close to them. From time to time, the song broke off in a screech as one of them cut her hand deeper than usual. Most cuts they hardly noticed: it happened so often, and the brine they worked in hardened them, eventually. Their fingers were scarred all over.

Freefield was not one dock but many: a small town of wharves, stores, curing-houses and boat-building yards just outside Lerwick. It was Shetland's first real industrial enterprise, Hay and Ogilvy's testament of faith in a future of free trade, the prospect that had so excited Kirstie's James. And in 1839 it was, undeniably, an exciting place to be: one had a sense of being where everything was happening; where the future was being made. Christian Ployen, for one, couldn't keep away from it. He had an excuse, since he was meant to be studying its operations, but it was not duty that took him down there so often to taste its air.

A well-dressed young Shetlander came in, and Ployen forced some of the eagerness and interest out of his face. He was the Governor of the Faroe Islands, not a tourist, and he had no wish to seem like the country boy at the fair, even if he felt like him. The young man was in his mid-twenties, with an engaging smile. Ployen knew him from somewhere.

"Governor Ployen, Uncle Charles sends his apologies; he is detained at business and I am to entertain you a while."

Ployen smiled graciously, and racked his brains for who this was. "Uncle Charles" had to be Charles Ogilvy, his host in Shetland, so this was a nephew, which was little help because he recalled meeting at least half a dozen. Ever since he arrived in Lerwick, he had been enveloped in the compulsive hospitality of the Shetland gentry. They seemed to be determined to make up for being a small, isolated group in the population by having large families, among whom they passed guests round as a matter of course; and all the families were inter-related by marriage. He knew now that he should, from the start, have tried to keep some kind of record of them all: as things were, he was frequently baffled.

He followed the young man out of the yard, past the risqué banter of the fish-gutters — Ployen was a tall, fair man, and his embarrassment always amused them. But his companion replied, good-humouredly, in their own style. Nephew ... which nephew? He tried to recall, and listen to the man's chat at the same time. As they passed the old fort, where the sheriff-court was now held, the young man stopped and called to someone coming out of the gate.

"You will have met my brother Andrew the lawyer?"

The Governor reflected ruefully that he might well have done. This Andrew looked considerably older than his brother, but with families of ten or twelve being nothing out of the ordinary, that could well be. He had a shrewd, clever face, a lawyer's face right enough, Ployen thought, until he noticed the humour and kindness in the eyes. They were amused and quizzical: Ployen felt sure they had read his face.

"It might be of more help to his excellency, Charlie, if ye said Andrew Duncan", the newcomer observed to his brother; then turning to Ployen, "and when we met at Mr Ogilvy's he was introducing you to the half of Lerwick, whom you 've surely now forgotten to a man." He smiled, and Ployen returned it gratefully.

"I must with shame, indeed, confess that I had," he said in his formal, correct English, "and now I am the more confused, for this gentleman is Mr Charles Duncan, Mr Ogilvy's nephew, and I thought I had met him already, but it was another."

"Oh, that 'll be Charles Gilbert," said the young man, "did he take you trout-fishing?"

"He did, and I shocked him very greatly by asking why we could not take them with nets, which seemed easier. But his name was Gilbert, then?"

Andrew laughed. "Governor Ployen, we're a most provoking breed: there are too many of us and we show no invention in our names. Also we call each other uncle and nephew and much else on insufficient provocation. Charlie and I, and a horde of others, are the children of Andrew Duncan the Sheriff-Substitute[6], who has probably stayed in your memory longer than we did, with perfect justice. And Andrew has a brother, Gilbert, whom you may know since he is married to Charles Ogilvy's sister?" Ployen nodded: he was keeping up so far.

"Well, Andrew's son is Gilbert Charles, known to us as Charlie to distinguish him from Uncle Gilbert .... Ye'd best attend closely here, sir, it gets awful complicated. So when, a few years later, Uncle Gilbert called his son Charles Gilbert, we had to call him it in full to know him from this scapegrace.. He ruffled his young brother's hair. "The same Charles Gilbert, who took you angling, is really Mr Ogilvy's nephew. We, I suppose, are not ... but Elizabeth Ogilvy is married to Uncle Gilbert, so she's our aunt, and what can our aunt's brother be but our uncle? It's a friendly way of reasoning, and provides us with all the relatives we need, but it drives strangers fair daft."

Ployen smiled again. He had been some weeks in Shetland now, and he knew there were points on which he disagreed with his hosts; but they were an engaging bunch. Even men of business like Charles Ogilvy and William Hay, energetic as they were in the office, had outside it an easy-going generosity to which it was hard not to respond. He liked their obvious joy in their large families, and the way they managed to run the town by doing several jobs at once — Charles Ogilvy, when not doing business or being chief magistrate, was the Danish consul, which was how he came to be Ployen's host. He liked their enthusiasm for their town: with reservations, he liked the town. It was still on a human scale, still small enough not to overwhelm one. (He thought with a shudder of the great granite mass of Aberdeen, to which his researches into the fishing industry had also taken him.)

They were in Commercial Street now, the long paved road that followed the curve of the foreshore from Fort Charlotte southwards round to the old Tolbooth. To all intents, this was the town, this and the dozens of narrow lanes that branched off it on the landward side, climbing the steep slope up to the road called Hillhead. It was an endearingly unplanned sort of street, each man having built his house as and where it suited him, so that the line was totally uneven and the street wide and narrow by turns. The narrow places meant there could be no wheeled traffic bigger than a small cart, but since there were scarcely any roads outside Lerwick, it hardly mattered. The little ponies came down it though, laden with their baskets of peat; Ployen was used to flattening himself against walls.

6 "Sheriff-Substitute" : The Sheriff Principal for both Orkney and Shetland was based in Orkney.

He gathered that they were going to Andrew's house for dinner. Nobody had actually said so; it was the sort of thing that happened as a matter of course: you ran into someone who was a distant connection of your host's, so he fed you. There was quite a good hotel in Lerwick, but Ployen often felt it had no chance of staying in business. He held his breath as they left the Street and plunged into the network of narrow, interconnecting lanes.

God knew, the dirt and refuse in the Street were bad enough, unless the municipal scavengers had just been down it, but the lanes were far worse. The main problem was that the town, quite simply, had no sewage system. There was a dunghill on every corner, sometimes every few yards, and in the enclosed lanes the stench could be appalling. Out of politeness to his hosts, Ployen resolutely pretended not to notice, but Andrew and Charlie had no such compunctions and complained wryly all the way up the steep hill. It was an unspeakable relief to close Andrew's front door on it.

Ployen settled back in his chair and stared down into his faceted crystal glass. The red wine glowed in it, smelling of fruit. It was a heavy glass, cool and pleasant to hold. His other hand, straying over a side-table, rested on a book bound in Levant morocco, with gold clasps. He looked at young Charlie, lounging in his fashionable clothes; Andrew, at ease in the midst of beautiful things, and shook his head, baffled.

"Yes, it puzzles me", he acknowledged Andrew's raised eyebrow. "I saw some poor streets in Aberdeen, but the gentlefolk did not live in them, nor have to see them much; they lived in better parts of the town, or outside it, and they had made their surroundings as they liked to have them. But here .... perhaps a few live outside, like Mr Ogilvy at Seafield, but the most of you are in the heart of it, in lanes like these. I had thought, at first, it must needs be a good thing, for if the folk with the money had to see such things, they would soon make a change to them."

"Instead of which we shut our house doors on them? Aye, we do that; though in justice to ourselves I don't know that we can do any other. The cleaning of the town is in the hands, or more properly the three dozen brooms, of the Police Commissioners, and they've not the means to do more — why, they raise a rate of sixpence in the pound as it is, and if they asked the kind of money that would make drains and sewers, the burgesses would be taken with a seizure."

"Why cannot the Town Council do something?"

Andrew laughed. "Because it was set up with a fine charter from His Majesty, (telling us we were a Burgh of Barony, extending from the sea even as far as the west boundary of Robert Hughson's kailyard), and it had a Town Clerk, and the noblest of intentions, but what it had not was money, nor the means of raising any, for nobody gave it power to levy rates. So it issues proclamations, and loyal addresses affirming its attachment to the Crown, in case the Crown should have been in doubt of it. Sam Henry is good at that."

"Those feelings of patriotic regard..." intoned Charlie solemnly, and Andrew took it up with him: clearly it was a family joke: "... are cherished even in the isles ..."

"... of Ultima Thule", they finished together, trying to keep straight faces.

Ployen smiled. "I remember Mr Henry. He was a very dignified man, I thought, and very proud of his office as the Town Clerk. If he is proud of the town, and wishes it to have dignity and honour in the world, that is not so strange?"

"Och, I was meaning no harm of Sam," said Andrew easily, "he's one of our own kind after all. Only, if you asked my father or Uncle Gilbert what would make them proud of the town ... they would tell you maybe clean streets, or an end to the typhus fever, or folk not needing to beg at their doors of a Saturday. And Arthur Anderson would say more schooling for the bairns; and Charles Ogilvy would say yet more work at Freefield, and men making their own living instead of being tied to the lairds .... What manner of a town do you want Torshavn to be?"

"I don't know. I wonder sometimes if anyone will have a choice ... did anyone truly plan for Aberdeen or Edinburgh to be as they are? Perhaps it is a thing men cannot direct, — as you say that you can do nothing about your streets. But all the same, I think if men can make things as they wish, it must be now, when the town is still of a size for a few men to make a difference to it. Freefield will make many people rich, I think: there will be the money to do almost anything to the town, if that is what they choose to spend it on — I mean people like your father and uncle, and Mr Henry, and the merchants like Mr Ogilvy and Mr Hay."

"And Charles Gilbert," Andrew remarked, lighting his pipe, "don't be forgetting him."

"What, the young man who took me fishing?" Ployen was puzzled. "Why, he can hardly have been twenty."

"Twenty-three," said Andrew, "but that's no' the point." He blew a smoke-ring at Charlie. "Very formidable, is our cousin. Folk like Charlie and me here ken fine what we want, but if we canna get it, we'll settle for a quiet life. Charles Gilbert is different". He smiled, a little ironically. "Did you forget his face, when you'd met him the once?"

Ployen thought back to the rainy day at the loch, and the pearly sea-trout, and the young man whose face was so still and grave until he smiled.

"No," he said, a little surprised, "no, I hadn't."

Chapter 6
Lerwick: January, 1840

Almost since the first day she and James arrived in Lerwick, Kirstie had been afraid. It wasn't an altogether unpleasant feeling; sometimes indeed it more resembled excitement, even exhilaration, but at the back of it was fear, of a place which was so far outside her experience that she had no frame of reference for it, and where what could happen to you, both for good and bad, was almost without limit.

James had told her things about it, that he himself had heard from friends. About the paved street, with houses both sides, and the dozens of shops (she had never seen more than one, in any one place, and was secretly puzzled as to how there could be enough goods to put in them all). But nothing could have prepared her for standing in Commercial Street, the November morning they came into town, looking up and up at three-storey buildings that leaned towards each other across the narrow street as if they meant to crush her. Underfoot was stone: to either side, and ahead, and behind, and up into the sky. Her throat had constricted, and she came close to turning and running. She had hugged the baby in her shawl more tightly instead, and clutched at James' arm with her other hand.

"Du's nae need to be fear'd, lass." James took care not to let his voice show how shaken he was himself. He had thought he was prepared for it, but he knew now that he had never really imagined anything but a bigger version of a crofting settlement. This wasn't just bigger, it was totally different. A man in a red cap stopped him, to ask directions, he supposed, and he was about to say that he was a stranger here himself, when he realised that nothing the man had said made any sense to him. He stood blank-faced, and the man tried again, just as incomprehensibly. Then someone across the street called a reply, and he went off grinning. James hadn't understood a word of it.

It came to him quite quickly: they had been Dutch or German or whatever; he knew there was plenty of foreign trade in Lerwick. But just for a moment, before common sense replaced panic, he had thought it was the language of the town, and the place was so alien that he hadn't been surprised. He shivered slightly, and Kirstie's nails dug more deeply into his arm, her eyes wide as a rabbit's caught in a light.

Her eyes had stayed like that, dilated and terrified, all the way down the street, and up the lane where they were to lodge. Only when they were finally in the room, and James had at last put down the heavy sea-chest that held most of what they owned, and she had been sitting on it a while feeding the baby, did her face return to something like calm.

Looking back on it, Kirstie could almost smile at her terror. She was part of the life of the place now, beginning to know how things were done. The things that were the same as in her former life, like climbing the hills at the back of the town to get peat for the fire. And the things that weren't, like queuing at the well or buying milk at a shop instead of going to the byre for it. She knew now what they needed all the shops for; it had never occurred to her how many of the daily needs of life were produced on the crofts. She used a little white basin to bring the milk home in: it was one of the first things she had bought in Lerwick, or rather exchanged for her knitting.

She loved the shops. Because so many people were at work all day, they kept open late at night even in winter, though they had only the flickering fish-oil lamps to defy the dark with. You would stumble down the street, in the shadows between the faint gleams of light, hoping you hadn't stepped in anything too obnoxious, and the near-dark would be full of people. Women just out of Freefield's gutting sheds, a day's work already behind them, dragging themselves round the shops to get some food in, before going back to the infants they hadn't seen since morning. Sailors off whatever ships were in, the quiet Dutchmen, or the wild boys from the Greenland whalers intent on getting drunk. The girls who hung around where the sailors were. The gentlefolk, criss-crossing the little town to each others' nightly dances and card-parties — outside Lerwick they could use ponies or carriages but within the network of narrow lanes they had to get about as everyone else did, and Kirstie would wish for more light to admire their fashions. Children, wandering the streets while their parents worked. On the croft, the rhythms of life followed the light. While it lasted, you worked; when it failed, you went indoors and prepared, soon enough, for sleep. To turn night into day, for her, had been something special and occasional: here they did it all the time, casually, as if day and night were something they would decide for themselves.

Superficially, her occupations had not altered much. She still ran the household, spun, knitted. Only now the wool was not pulled[7] from the sheep: you got it from the merchant, who deducted the price of it from the finished article when he bought it back from you. She missed the closeness to animals a little: the warmth and comforting stolidity of cows, the dependence of the house-bred lambs or piglets she and Mary had played mother to. Little Jamie got all of that, now. He was about

7 "pulled" : The loose wool of Shetland sheep was combed or pulled rather than shorn.

27

sixteen months old, too big really to carry around as much as she did, but she did not like to be apart from him. He and James were what she had brought from home — that and a bed, a loom, a spinning-wheel and Hercules' old sea-chest.

James was working at the loom until the fishing season started. He had a promise of work, on a boat owned by Mr Linklater the merchant, who bought Kirstie's knitting and spinning, or rather exchanged it for goods. It was no different from at home, really, except that there were more merchants to choose from. But they all dealt the same way: you were still stuck with selling your goods, and buying theirs, at the price they set. And knitting and spinning, being women's work, would never be priced high. Kirstie was an industrious, quick worker and James was always full of praise for her help with the family finances, but they both knew she could never pay the rent. Only James could do that, and even he had trouble when there was only the weaving.

But the fishermen were paid in cash, and a season of good catches would give them not only the rent but enough to put some by, to get ahead of the game at last. That was what they could never have done on their hungry northern croft, and why they had come to Lerwick. For James, it was still the land of opportunity.

Kirstie's feelings were more mixed. She shared some of his excitement, and it was true that some amazing things could happen to you in a place like this. There was James' friend Jimmy Hunter, who had first started him thinking about Lerwick. He had just been a fisherman then, like themselves; now he was some gentleman's agent and managed his property: he even collected James and Kirstie's rent. There were rich merchants in Lerwick who had started as little more than day-labourers[8]. On the croft, change took generations. She had known what her life would be like, having seen her mother's and grandmother's. Down in Commercial Street, or by the harbour with Jamie, watching the ships unload fancy goods from down south and hearing the babble of languages, she could sense how much faster things happened here. It was a heady feeling, the nearest she would ever be to getting drunk, and she loved it.

Only there was another side to the place. The first thing that had struck her about the lanes had been the nauseating filth. Back on the croft, if weather made it impossible to go any distance from the house, there was always the byre: here the best that could be managed was a screened-off bucket in the room, emptied periodically on to a midden, under the eyes, not to say the noses, of the populace. But there were worse things about the streets than that. The drunken whalers, for one: paralytic if you were lucky; riotous and violent if you weren't. And something which frightened her more: people, quiet, patient people,

8 "day-labourers" : The most notable being Arthur Anderson, founder of the P&O Shipping Line.

quite ordinary people like her and James, who didn't seem to have any homes to go to and slept out at night. There was Saturday, begging day, when these same patient people queued outside the doors of the gentry hoping for food and clothes. She couldn't help thinking that they had maybe been like Jimmy Hunter too, when they came to Lerwick; just fisherfolk. And the town could do this to you, too.

So she lived from day to day in a state of apprehension, sometimes hopeful, sometimes fearful, and constantly surprised; venturing out to taste the excitement of the place and retreating, when it got too big for her, to the room. The room was all-important: small, predictable and safe, the only part of her world which seemed to be on the same scale as she was.

Since she and James had only been in town a couple of months when Christmas came around, they knew hardly anyone and were resigned to celebrating quietly in the room with Jamie. But late on Christmas eve, Jimmy Hunter called round and suggested they come out with him. Kirstie hesitated.

"It's ower caald fir da bairn."

"Row him in dy shawl, lass. Lerook on Yule e'en's a bonnie sicht."

Down on the Street, the shops still had their lamps glimmering, and some were burning candle as well. Kirstie recalled at once the blazing breakfast-time once a year in the croft. There were a great many children out, some with lamps or makeshifts, like a candle in a jar, and to her surprise they were in fancy dress. They were singing, dancing, clowning, knocking at every house and shop door as they passed, and at most doors they were given money.

"Dat's da peerie guizers," Jimmy told her, "dey'll be gane hame sune." She watched them, enchanted.

Groups of young men began to gather on the street corners, their faces full of suppressed excitement, like little boys plotting something. Some, like the children, wore masks and costumes. A knot of much older men stood by the Market Cross, looking anxious.

The children had melted away, and Kirstie asked if they should go now. Jimmy laughed and shook his head, and the Tolbooth clock began to sound midnight.

On the last stroke, James and Kirstie thought for a moment that the town had exploded. From every direction came the crack of pistol shots, and the deeper sound of seven-pounders. Jamie wailed, and Kirstie hid him in her shawl, but his voice was lost in the din.

One of the groups of young men ran up Baker's Closs. The older men followed, half-reluctantly, it seemed. Almost as soon as they were out of sight, another band of youngsters appeared from further down the Street. They were hauling a great wooden sledge with three or four barrels on it. The barrels were all alight and blazing like fury; the reek of burning tar carried on the salty wind. It lit up the Street in garish, unnatural colours.

There was a roar, and another blazing sledge burst out of the lanes, towed by the men who'd vanished up Baker's Closs. They swung left into the Street, too fast, and one of the barrels fell off and burst in the road, sending up showers of sparks. The young men cheered, and one of them threw something on the flames. The explosion was quite minor, really: a brief blinding flash and a few windows broken. Jimmy Hunter laughed, and James, uncertainly, with him.

The elderly special constables panted down the lane and gazed, ruefully, at the sledges disappearing in opposite directions down the Street. There was another glow now, from high up near Hillhead. Some of them trudged off up the hill towards it, but most gave up and joined the crowd of onlookers.

The young guizers raced the sledges up and down the Street, with a crowd running alongside. When the flames began to die down, they stirred the molten tar with long poles and stimulated matters with gunpowder firecrackers. Kirstie thought: Trafalgar must have been like this; and felt slightly guilty, never having been sure how much of Hercules' tales to believe.[9] (One of her few disappointments in Lerwick had been the trees. There were some, in the rich folks' gardens, but they were meagre and wind-stunted, little taller than the overgrown bushes she had seen up north, and certainly not the vast, house-high, singing avenue of her imagination. James thought maybe the tall ones grew further south still, but she wondered if they existed at all.)

The sledges burned out, in the end, on the stone piers by the sea; the image of their torches glinting red on the water under a dark winter sky. It was about seven in the morning: James and Kirstie walked home along the Street where house doors stood wide to entertain the guizers, while a few enterprising merchants opened in hopes of trade from the onlookers, and others, muttering, came out to assess the damage to their windows. Jamie was wide awake. Kirstie had baked the Yule-brunnies the night before, and they had saved candle for the feast of light.

But it would look pale now, she thought, after the savage fire. Flames roof-high, a whole street bright as day in the dead of winter: what compared with that were candle-ends on a table, or an old man carrying a light?

9 "Trafalgar" : It has been suggested that the riotous Yuletide festival in Lerwick was inspired less by Viking times than by the 1815 peace celebrations.

Chapter 7
Lerwick: Tuesday, 10th February, 1840

Commercial Street ran parallel to the shoreline, so the high buildings gave some shelter from the wind blowing off the sea. But it seemed to lurk at the corners, ready to surprise you: sudden gusts spitting a fine, icy rain.

It was scarcely unusual weather for February, but Samuel Henry still felt faintly annoyed. It was unsuitable for a Queen's wedding day; vaguely disrespectful. Also he was worried about the lights. He had them fixed all the way down the Street, wicks burning fish-oil in glass lanterns; the town would be illuminated, come nightfall, just like so many others across the kingdom. He was proud of that: it mattered to him that what the mainland could do, so could this speck of island out in the North Sea. Ultima Thule. He had sent off another loyal address to the Crown, to mark the occasion, and proclamations had been posted up in the Street forbidding any tar-barrels or home-made fireworks. Henry wanted a decorous celebration, not another fiery rampage like Yule and New Year.

He was one of the few who really hated to see the sledges burn on the piers. Even the special constables usually didn't try too hard to stop it, and felt the same atavistic delight at that blaze in the darkness as the lads with the torches. But it kindled nothing in him. For one thing, he found it savage and crude. There was a vein of refinement in him; things like fine paper, and sonorous language, and his own exquisite handwriting, gave him a sensual pleasure which was keen, yet not wild nor uncontrolled. Sometimes indeed, when he sang in church or listened to his daughters at the piano, he felt how, if he let it, the music could sweep him away on a tide of feeling, beyond all reason, as the fire did to those savages in the streets. But he chose not to let it.

Anyway, the sledges with their burning barrels were a defiance of authority; if they got to the piers intact, it meant anarchy had won for the night. He would have gone to great lengths to stop them, simply because of that.

He decided to check that his notices, further down the Street, had not been interfered with. On the way he nodded to Linklater the merchant, busy in his shop, and then clutched hastily at his hat as another gust of wind caught him.

Linklater was in a good mood. Many of the gentlefolks had parties planned for tonight, so the merchants had been doing a brisk trade in provisions. Outside the fishing season, when the poorer people had less to spend, something like this made a big difference. A couple of women came in with knitting and spinning to sell him, and he greeted them genially. One of them had a little boy, about eighteen months, who tried to reach up to the brightly coloured sweets on the counter.

"Na, na." His mother pulled him away gently. Linklater reached into the jar and took a couple of sweets out. "There's fir ye, me lad." He waved the woman's thanks away: "Hit's no' every day dat da Queen mairries."

"Whit Queen's dat?" the woman asked, mildly interested. She was young, dark-haired, with a slightly wide-eyed look, like one to whom everything is still new. She was very watchful of the boy.

"Save us, da Queen in London! Wis du never heard o her?"

The woman thought a moment. "Aye", she said slowly; "she cam ta be Queen tree years fae syne."

"Aye, near enough."

"I wis mairrit ta James dat year," she said quietly, smiling. "I mind we wir in da new place, awa' fae me folk, an' a neebir telt me da Queen wis had ta leave her midder an' set up hoosekeepin' forbye."

Linklater laughed. "Aye, she did that. Weel, she's mairryin' the day; she'll maybe sune have a bonny bairn like wee Jamie."

Kirstie smiled again, this time with intense pride. "Gude keep her," she said, eyes still fixed on Jamie, "who's she mairryin'?"

Mr Linklater was busy with his stock again. "Some German, I think," he called over his shoulder.

Kirstie had seen a fair few Germans; their ships often traded at Lerwick. It seemed odd to think of the Queen marrying one of those stolid merchants or hard-faced blond sailors. But of course, a Queen's husband would be different. Rich and handsome, probably. She felt no envy: indeed she was smiling inwardly, hoping for the Queen's sake that the German was as good in bed as James Jamieson. It would be nice, though, never to have to worry about the rent.

The gentry of Lerwick spent most of the night in and out of each others' houses, cruising from party to party. At a late hour, Andrew Duncan ended up in his father's house, feeling pleasantly sleepy. His father and uncle, and the other elderly gents, were chatting by the fire; the young folk were dancing or courting. He was forty: like most men he thought of himself as younger and felt he must belong with the dancers, but he knew, ruefully, that he preferred the idea of the fire. He sipped his wine, and watched both groups. One of the young men, too enthusiastic in his dancing or possibly not completely sober, bumped into him and apologised.

"A great loun like yourself," said Andrew severely, "should be out with the special constables, keepin' the peace."

There was a gust of laughter, and the young man grinned and blushed. His name was Sinclair Goudie, and four years earlier he *had* been a special, drafted in to help stop the annual barrel-burning. It was a particularly wild Yule that year: Sinclair finished it in jail, having been arrested for setting off gunpowder firecrackers. The Commissioners of Police had not called on his services since.

More than one voice invited Andrew to join them, but he smiled and shook his head. He was popular with young folk for his sense of humour and lack of any inclination to preach or domineer: he always had been. He just wasn't one of them any more. He noticed a man he knew, standing apart like himself, and strolled over to him.

"Is Mrs Angus no wií you?"

William Angus was about Andrew's age. He shook his head: "She was, but she's away home to her bed a while fae syne. Nae doubt, da morn , I'll wish I'd done the same."

Andrew laughed. "Aye, Catherine guid home too." They drank companionably, against the background of fiddle music and young ringing voices, and the murmur from the fireside. At one point the old men got more animated; voices were raised and William Angus grinned.

"They'll be putting the town to rights again", he observed.

Andrew listened a moment. "No, I think it's just the world. If it was the town they were talking about, there would likely be more argument, and louder voices."

"Aye, ye could be right." William gestured towards the dancers. "If I can ever get yon lasses o' mine to laeve, I'll be for home. I'm no' young enough to keep dis hours."

Andrew's eyes followed his. "They're bonny lasses, your daughters ... is there no' one missing?"

"Aye, Margaret's no' there. She was away to visit some auld body, when we left; she said she'd be along later. But like enough she's cuttin' up my shirts for bandages. Gude kens ... if she was here, she'd doubtless be raising a subscription to send someone's bairn to the school."

Andrew smiled. "Come, she's a good lass and you'd no' have her different. Or them, either."

William did manage, eventually, to bustle his daughters out. Andrew watched their teasing familiarity with a feeling of pain.

He was one of twelve children, but he had none. As he grew older, he was drawn more and more to the young, but his casual popularity with them was a world away from William's intimacy with his daughters, or the deep bond he felt with his own father. More than anything, he wanted to recreate that; to be to a son what his father had been to him. But he was prepared to envy even those whose children had died in infancy. Having younger brothers, sisters, cousins, nephews, nieces gave him an outlet for his affections, but it did nothing to stop him feeling there was a void inside him, growing wider by the year. Sometimes he wondered if it was why he had never taken such an energetic part in the town's life as his father and uncle. He could see, as they did, the problems of poverty and disease and uncleanliness. But where they argued energetically on the Town Council and the Police Commission about how to mend matters with plainly inadequate resources, he tended to stand back and smile wryly at their intenseness.

True, he had often given his time and expertise free to people who couldn't afford to pay for legal advice. But it didn't seem much. He thought of young Margaret Angus and her zeal for working among the poor. She would be expecting to marry one day, and have children: it mattered to her what the town would come to be like, as it mattered to his father, and to Uncle Gilbert with his ten children, and to Charles Ogilvy and William Hay with their equally large broods.

But to him? He honestly didn't know. It seemed to him that he believed in the ideals his friends and family held; that he wanted the same things for the town. But he could sense no intensity in himself when he thought about it. If he tried to visualise the town's future, there was nothing of him in it, no line stretching from him to connect him with it. He was a stander-aside.

He wandered over to the fire, to listen to the old men. They were talking now about getting an old croft on the Knab, a windswept headland just outside town, converted for a fever hospital. There were always fevers: every year something virulent seemed to break out. One of the old men was blaming the foreign boats for bringing it in, but the Sheriff, Andrew's father, was roundly disagreeing: the doctors, he said, were convinced it was the filth in the streets, and in many of the houses.

They had been having this conversation since the outbreak of '37, which had looked especially likely to spread and had thoroughly alarmed even the wealthy, who recalled family stories from the last century, when the smallpox would sweep through every twenty years and take ten children at a time from the highest families in the islands. At least, now, you could be vaccinated against that, though many of the poor still weren't, but there was no such cure for the fever, and no means of stopping its spread except by isolation. Of course the problem, as usual, was money: they all wanted the hospital but far fewer wanted to pay rates to the Police Commissioners to get it going. In the end, Andrew guessed, private charity would have a lot to do with it: someone like Arthur Anderson would reach into his pocket yet again.

And the thought nudged him, uncomfortably, that the Andersons were childless, too.

When he went home, the old men's chat was still as lively as ever; they enjoyed an argument hugely. The young folk, too, were glad of an excuse for a dance, so all in all the Queen's wedding day was a popular success. It even turned out well from Samuel Henry's point of view, for the weather about which he had been so anxious at least discouraged the lads from burning any barrels or setting off any gunpowder. It was a decorous, contained, law-abiding celebration, a credit to his administration and to Ultima Thule in general. The only thing, he reflected, that could have made him happier would have been an assurance that all the town's festivals would be like that.

Mr Linklater did good trade all day, even after dark when folk came out to look at the little lights. He spent the day, in consequence, in a rattling good humour and gave a better rate for the knitting than usual.

So it was a good day for Kirstie, as well, because she had a little cash to put aside for the rent.

Chapter 8
Lerwick: Tuesday, 9th September, 1840

A shaft of light struck through the small, uncurtained window, and Kirstie stirred in the bed against James. She tried to cuddle up to him, and then remembered why it felt awkward: she was four months pregnant. On the other side of her, little Jamie stirred, sighed and curled up again, like a cat.

James turned toward her, still half asleep, and held her for a few moments. Then he grunted resignedly and got out of bed, quietly, so as not to wake the boy. Kirstie heard him at the hearth, coaxing the fire back into life. She made to get up herself.

"Na, bide where du is, lass, du's no' got ta geeng ta da fishin'"

"Is da wedder fair?"

"Aye, it's no' lookin' ill." He began to make tea, but she stretched out her arms to him. He shook his head, smiling, and gestured at the boy.

"He winna stir", she said, hardly above a whisper. James hesitated, then came back over to the bed.

Nothing in her life had surprised her as much as the pleasure she got out of James' body. No child grows up on a farm without learning how male and female come together, but the casual matings of animals had nothing to do with pleasure, certainly not for the females. The cock might scream in triumph and shake his feathers into a shiver of redness: the hen merely moved off and went on feeding. The ponies on the skyline fused for a moment into a single humped, ungainly silhouette, then parted as if nothing had happened. Even the surreptitious rustles and creaks from Hercules' and Margaret's bed on the other side of the dark room ended in stifled grunts that sounded more like pain than anything else.

Twenty-four years of sharing a bed with sisters were poor preparation for being next to a body she could not touch without excitement. Sliding her hand under wool or cotton, (no-one took off more than their outer clothes to go to bed), she would come on flesh, and it was like putting your hand on something charged with static. She liked it in winter best, when they could hardly see each other's bodies, and must know them only by touch. Even then she would close her eyes, screwing them tighter and tighter to see deep blues and reds, until the light exploded behind them.

They had to go carefully now, to avoid waking Jamie, but stealth, the feeling that their pleasure was something secret and stolen, merely heightened it. Afterwards she still didn't want to let him get up.

"Da boat 'll no' wait for me, lass, an' Martinmas isna a' dat far."

She let his arms go. Martinmas was 11th November, when the rent was due.

It was clear to everyone in Lerwick now that something was happening to the cod and herring fishing that had built Freefield dock, put money in men's pockets and goods in the shops. For the last couple of years, catches had been light, and this summer had been no better. But now the whitefish were over, it was time for the herring, and she knew James and his mates were hopeful of some decent catches to end the season. They needed them. A lot of people were behind with the rent, and the Jamiesons were among them.

He was gone very quickly, slipping out into the morning before the child awoke. Kirstie made some more tea and thought about the rent. If James' wages didn't cover it by Martinmas, she might have to ask to be paid for her knitting in cash rather than in goods. But you got less that way, and no merchant would give you all of it in cash.

She slipped out to empty the bucket while Jamie was still asleep. By the time she got back, he had woken: she made gruel from oatmeal and they ate it together. He was two now, and talking quite a lot; she found herself singing him the songs and rhyme-games Hercules had taught her.

She finished a pair of stockings, and put them aside with the others to take to Linklater. Not yet. It was full day now, and if she didn't get to the well soon, there would be a queue.

It stood in Mounthooly Street, which ran down the hill to Commercial Street. Mounthooly was paved, and quite wide by comparison with the lanes. The reason for the flagstones was a stream that ran the length of the street and down to the sea; hidden under the stones now, but sometimes it would get blocked and overflow, claiming its space back. It was a peat burn, its waters brown and muddy, and all the more so when they had swept the street's rubbish up with them. But there wasn't much flooding there today, Kirstie noted with relief. When the street was awash, and they had a long wait at the well, it was difficult to stop Jamie playing in the filthy water.

Kirstie knew most of the folk at the well, not that many were there yet. A young servant girl from one of the big houses in nearby Sheriff's Closs, who played with Jamie. Ann Goodlad, whom Kirstie felt sorry for because her husband was in a hospital for crippled sailors somewhere down south, so that she might as well have been a widow.

Young Laurina, about eight, with her even younger brother: they were orphans and lived with their big brother Alex, who was all of fifteen. Kirstie wondered how far behind their rent was.

"Is Alex gane ta da fishin' dis mornin', Laurie?"

The child shook her head. "He cudna get work. Hit's no' fair, a bonny day like dis whin da herrin'll come easy."

Kirstie and Ann shushed her automatically: it was bad luck to say things like that, and might keep the fish away.

It was hard work getting back up the steep lane, and the stairs to the room, with a heavy pail dragging on one arm and a tired child on the other. She put him down to sleep for a while, resumed her knitting and pondered whether to make tea again. She shouldn't really: it cost money and meant a trip to the well all the sooner. But like most of the women she knew, she loved the stuff: it revitalised them and made them feel ready for whatever life had to throw at them next.

By the time the child woke, she had a good pile of knitting to take to Linklater's. It was nearly noon: she fed him some more gruel and they set off again, down the lane and then up Commercial Street, with the boy wide-eyed, wanting his mother all the time to look at some sight in the street or in a shop window; she smiling and saying she'd seen it all before. There was a whaling ship in, on its way back from the north, and some of the sailors were in town. One of them loomed unsteadily over Kirstie and James, and she froze: she was still afraid of the whalers. But maybe this one was missing a family, for he stroked little Jamie's hair and gave him a couple of ship's biscuits.

At Linklater's, she bumped into Laurina again; the child was another of his knitters. He proved not to be in a particularly good mood. He complained about the quality of the knitting (which was no different from normal), and vowed he would be ruined if just one more person asked him for cash instead of goods. What was the matter with folk in this town: could they not put enough aside for their rent without expecting him to make a bank out of himself? In the end he estimated Kirstie's work at £3 in goods, and allowed her threepence of it in cash. Laurina, with fifteen shillings' worth, could get no cash out of him.

He did look genuinely preoccupied, and Kirstie wondered if he too was worried about the fishing. The boat-owner must suffer from low catches as well as the fishermen, she supposed, though she'd never seen one who seemed to be suffering. She thought of reminding him that the herring might make up for it, but it would have been unlucky, like Laurie's remark at the well.

It took a while to do the shopping, what with chatting to Laurie and coaxing Jamie away from things they couldn't afford. (Knitting was worth less if you asked cash for it, but oddly enough goods cost more when you bought them with knitting instead of cash. It was a good arrangement, for merchants.) Nonetheless she was surprised, when she came out, to see how much darker the sky was. She hadn't thought it could be so late, and said as much to Laurie.

"Hit's no' late", said Laurie, "da wedder's changed."

Kirstie realised at once that this was true. The darkness came from cloud, and not white cloud either but an ominous grey. A wind had sprung up, which she had not much noticed at first because it was blowing off the shore and they were relatively sheltered from it. At sea it would be a different matter. James was maybe due for a rough time.

She felt anxious, but she could hardly recall a day in her life, during the fishing season, when she hadn't felt anxious about someone — Hercules, or Robert, or James himself. If you let your mind dwell on it, you would never get anything done.

So they went home, and she tidied the shopping away and put the threepence aside for the rent, and then sat down to some spinning while Jamie slept again. Later she cooked fish and potatoes, and saved some for James. And Jamie ate a bun she shouldn't really have bought him (he was doing well today, what with the ship's biscuits) and played with a little wooden boat his father had made him. James was good with his hands. At weaving, and carpentry, and making love ... Her pregnancy made her feel slower than usual, as nearly idle as anyone in her position could afford to be. The bucket needed emptying again, but she didn't fancy the trip downstairs and back up. If James were here, he would do it for her, and for a moment she considered leaving it till he got home. Then she thought how exhausted he would be, especially if the weather had been bad, and she picked up the bucket and hauled it downstairs.

In the narrow, stuffy lane it was hard to tell what the weather was like, but she could hear loose shutters clapping somewhere: evidently the wind had not let up. She looked up at the sky: it was black as winter, so dark that on the way back from the midden she almost stumbled over a soft heap which stirred and muttered, and shrank back against the wall. She shivered, and quickened her pace. The room, when she got back, seemed warmer and more welcoming. She straightened the counterpane on the bed, her hands lingering where James had lain, and thought about sleeping out in that darkness, with no roof or walls around you, and no door to shut. Country folk believed there were trows and bogles in the dark, but she wasn't sure if they had power in a town. She mended the fire, and put the kollie lamp in the window, where it would give James some light.

It was some time later that she began to hear noise and movement outside. She thought at first that it was some of the whalers, on a rampage, but they didn't sound drunk, or aggressive. She stepped out on to the landing and saw women, on the stairs and coming out of the other rooms, their shawls over their heads.

"Whit is it?" she asked, and a woman on the stairs called back over her shoulder: "Da boats is wrackit."

Kirstie ran back into the room, threw on her shawl and caught up James. Soon they were part of the stream of women and children pouring down the stairs, and then along the steep lane; looking in their drab colours not unlike the Mounthooly burn breaking over the stones and flowing down to the sea. As they came out of the shelter of the lanes, a terrific wind hit them.

The harbour was crowded with people, trying to make out what was going on offshore, but between the darkness and the noise of the storm it was difficult to see or hear much. There were boats actually in the harbour, but helplessly out of control, and the sounds of splintering wood and screams rose now and then even above the hooting wind. Anything out at sea must be even worse off.

There were all sorts of people there: Kirstie saw Mr Linklater with his head in his hands, and some of the other merchants. But most of the crowd were women, many with infants huddled in their shawls. Some stood white-faced, biting their lips; some were crying. One sat slumped against a wall, hugging three toddlers to her and rocking rhythmically to and fro. Many of the children, woken from sleep, were fretful and wailing; they demanded over and over to know what was happening and where their fathers were. Jamie, mildly stimulated by all the excitement, caught the word "Dada", one of the ones he knew, and his face brightened: "Dada come?"

Kirstie did not reply. She stared out at the clashing black emptiness, thinking how, so lately, she had dreaded the idea of sleeping in the quiet, enclosed darkness of the lane. For the moment, her own situation and Jamie's did not concern her: she could think only of James not sleeping in his own bed on a night like this; hurled about for ever in the stinging spindrift; never getting warm.

A woman near her suddenly went into an hysterical panic, screaming over and over: "Whit'll we dae? Whit'll we dae?" A gentleman tried to calm her, explaining that nothing could be done; nobody could attempt a rescue in this. But the other women knew it was not what she had meant.

Eventually they mostly went home, the ones with children. Kirstie too, who held Jamie all night in the suddenly roomy bed and stared into the dark unsleeping, wide-eyed with fear, because she was thinking of herself and Jamie and the new baby, now. In the morning they went back to the shore, like everyone else. Some had stayed there all night.

The sea was quite calm now, and the air clear and fresh, as it often is after a storm. A black-clad clergyman was bustling up and down the beach consoling women, his arms flapping like the wings of a giant crow. The whole foreshore was strewn with wreckage, and people were

40

sifting about in it to find something that would identify the individual boats it came from. There were torn nets, and red caps, and everywhere spars, planks, the battered frames of boats like the ribs of whales, picked clean.

PART THREE

MARTINMAS

Chapter 9
Lerwick: 1841

Charles Ogilvy followed the sheriff's officer with the keys down the corridors of Fort Charlotte, looking and feeling ill at ease. He had shown a fair few guests round the courtroom and the other public offices in the fort, but this was the first who'd ever wanted to visit the cells. Ogilvy had things on his mind, but even in his more lighthearted days he might not have cared much for his current house guest.

He was a scientist called Wilson, working for the Board of Fisheries, and he was meant to be studying the herring industry. It was not obvious how one could do this by poking around the prison cells of Fort Charlotte, but that was typical of the man: he was as interested in people as he was in the herring, but only if he could get some entertainment out of them. He was slight, sickly and undeniably clever, with a permanently raised eyebrow and a quizzical, lazily amused air, as if he had come up to study the natives as much as the fish. Charles Gilbert Duncan, who as usual had been deputed to take him angling, was positively acid on the subject of Wilson, and his flippant cousin Charlie was perfecting an imitation of the man's refined Edinburgh drawl.

They went into one of the bare little cells, and an old man stood up to greet them. Ogilvy noticed with embarrassment that they had interrupted him in reading the Bible. Apart from the stool he had risen from, there was no other article of furniture in the room, so they all remained standing, while Wilson asked what the man had done.

"Aa wis stown twartree olliks," he said quietly, and Wilson turned to his host with overdone comic bafflement.

"Ling," said Ogilvy, "he stole two or three ling that were laid out drying. It lies out till it's hard dried, the ling, so it's aye a temptation."

"So that the fish cannot be out," observed Wilson, "but when the thieves are in." Ogilvy gave a token smile and shifted from foot to foot. Wilson went on drolling with, or at, the prisoner, but he was unresponsive; dispirited, as if he saw no help for anything. Ogilvy wondered whose fish the man had stolen: it might have been his for all he knew. It seemed a small crime to be locked up in the fort for; but there, it was the principle of the thing. If you let a small theft by, there'd be nothing safe, especially with times getting hard.

Wilson got bored with the lack of response, and they went to see the prisoner in the next cell. Ogilvy saw that the new specimen was a woman, and promptly excused himself on the ground of wanting some air. He didn't think he could listen to much more in the way of Wilson's humour.

Leaning on the ramparts, he stared down towards Freefield and thought about the four thousand-odd barrels stored there, waiting to be filled with fish. Wilson had seen them that morning, and raised that eyebrow of his, remarking that there wouldn't be much profit in them if the fishing failed.

He was right, of course, damn him. Hay and Ogilvy's great enterprise looked as busy and as vibrant now as it had looked two years back, when it fascinated Christian Ployen, but Ogilvy, gazing down on it, could see nothing but worry. The 1840 herring season had sunk with the thirty boats that went down on 9th September. Sixteen and a half thousand barrels ... he recalled wryly how poor he'd thought the season of '39. They hadn't even landed four and a half thousand in 1840.

Things were not desperate yet. Even now, a couple of good seasons would see them right ... maybe. If the Spanish would stop being awkward about exports, and if they could find new markets in Europe to replace the Indies. There were too many ifs, and the biggest concerned how long the Royal Bank of Scotland would go on carrying their overdraft.

The distant hammers of the coopers sounded unbearably light, as frivolous as Wilson's banter in the jail. The shrill laughter of the fish-gutters carried on the air: Ogilvy could hardly bear to listen to it. Freefield meant much more to him than a place of business. He was not fool enough to have tied up his personal assets with it: if it went down, he and his family would not starve. But even that was small consolation. All that life and activity down there had been his dream for his town, the way he wanted it to be. It was the work which would keep the young men at home, instead of at the whaling grounds of Greenland or the goldfields of California; it was the prosperity which would send their children to school and let them do better than their fathers. It was what even the likes of Wilson couldn't come up from the south and be condescending about. He and William Hay had started it because they wanted to get rich; he would never deny that was the main reason, but it wasn't the only one. Not for him, anyway.

He wondered how many people worked down there now, and realised he couldn't even make a guess. As for those who depended on it: the merchants who would lose trade because people couldn't afford their goods, the women whose knitting would fetch less, if they could sell it at all ... near enough the whole town, he supposed. Sometimes he wished he were more like his partner. William would have clapped him on the back and told him to make do with his own worries; everyone had to shift for themselves in this life. If Freefield went down, William Hay would be sorely annoyed, but it wouldn't break him. Maybe he would put a bit extra in the kirk collection for the poor, but he certainly would not lie awake wondering if he might be responsible for them.

Someone tossed a bucket of fish offal into the harbour, and the rancorous, scavenging gulls converged screaming on it. Please God, blow the bait in the fish's mouth this year. And make the Spaniards see sense, and give the Royal Bank the good gift of patience.

Margaret Angus picked her way up a narrow lane, trying to keep her skirts out of the mud. She had to climb nearly to the Hillhead to find the house she wanted, and then up a couple of flights of stairs. She rested a while to get her breath back, before knocking at the door; then she went in without waiting for an answer. A dark-haired, sallow woman was walking up and down feeding a baby, and knitting rapidly at the same time. On the floor, a boy of about three was playing, and tugging sometimes at her skirt.

"I sewed a bit dress for the bairn, Kirstie, out of an old shawl: look, it'll be grand and warm. I hope he's well?"

"Aye, he's daein' fine, thank you." Kirstie unlatched the baby and put him down on the bed. But he was about seven months old, and not feeling sleepy; he reached out with his hands, wanting to play. She called the boy: "Jamie, keep Mansie fir me." He seemed used to this; he came over and climbed on to the bed, chatting to the baby and playing with his fingers. Kirstie gestured Margaret to the chair and, still knitting, went to mend the fire. She asked over her shoulder: "Will I make some tea?"

The fire had gone low, and the room was chilly. There was a pile of dirty laundry beside the chair, too much to be the family's own; she must be taking in washing. Into the cold seeped a faint smell from the bucket in the corner. Margaret shivered.

"No, I canna stay lang. Du kens, Dr Cowie says the poor folk drink ower muckle tea, and it ruins their health?"

Kirstie laughed shortly. "Dr Cowie hasna his rent ta get wi' knittin' an' spinnin', an' twa bairns taiglin' roond at da sam time."

"Do you manage with the rent?"

Kirstie gave a half-shrug. "Sinclair Goudie's a kind man, he lets me pay some in wark. But it's no' easy."

Margaret knew it couldn't be. All the poor people she visited seemed to live in dread of the rent collector, especially the lone women with children, and the old folk past working. Rents were quite high in

Lerwick, and what the likes of Kirstie could earn by spinning and knitting wouldn't leave much to put aside after she had fed and clothed the children. Often, faced with someone plainly desperate about the rent, Margaret felt tempted to give them the money and be done with it. But all her own kind, even the most liberal-minded, agreed that this would never work. The poor were improvident; that was probably part of the reason they were poor. You couldn't rely on them to put money aside for Martinmas, or whenever else it would be needed: if they got it in their hand they would surely spend it on something less essential. So you had to help them with food and clothing.

Margaret was not altogether happy with this view of things, but going around so much among the poor did not make it easier to decide if there was anything better. Part of her sensed that the poverty often caused the improvidence, rather than the other way about: that people who had so little could not seriously expect to keep money around for long before a good use cropped up for it, and that some other need, like food or comfort, would always seem more urgent than the rent, until the day before Martinmas. She could feel even for the few (far fewer than some of her circle imagined) who spent money on drink; having seen where and how they lived.

Still, whatever had made them so, it was true enough that many of them couldn't hang on to money. At least Kirstie would not spend it on drink; Margaret knew she never touched the stuff. But there was always the tea, and, still more, the children: Kirstie indulged them, when she had the means, and would certainly never rate the landlord's claims above theirs.

Aside from all of which, there was the undoubted fact that if you started you would never stop: the town was full of deserving cases and she couldn't pay the rent for them all. Kirstie, actually, seemed to be keeping her head above water better than some. Her difficulty lay in being limited, by the infants and her own lack of any other skill, to low-paid indoor work. But she could do a lot of it; she was very industrious and she had her health. As long as she didn't have any more bad luck, she and the children should be all right. Margaret felt reasonably at ease about them, when she took her leave.

It was some weeks after this that a certain virus, which can survive a prodigious time outside the human body in some such friendly environment as laundry, gratefully took up a new residence. Kirstie had to stop and rest at the top of the stairs, which was rare indeed for her. Though her hands automatically picked up her knitting, she was slow with it; she felt feverish and every household task was a burden. Jamie and Mansie seemed twice as lively and demanding as usual: she found herself snapping at them and then regretting it. When the little one had gone to sleep, she mended the fire in an attempt to drive the shiver out of her bones, and cuddled Jamie, who looked puzzled to see her stop working for once. In the end he fell asleep too. She looked from him to the baby, wondering what would become of them if she had the typhus.

When the baby was born, she had thought for a long time about what to call him. Jamie had been named for his father's family; it would have been natural to name this one for her own. Hercules had died not long after she married and moved away. She felt it was he who had moved away first, so remote he had become. It was his old sea-chest she was sitting on now, rocking Jamie; she still recalled the times she had spent on it with Hercules, but in her mind the memory of the tall bringer of light was clouded with sorrow and resignation, a kind of brooding ineffectuality. It was from this that she had turned to James, looking for the fire and energy that had gone from her father. James had been the new life, as Lerwick was: even if it hadn't turned out as they had hoped, she felt she could never go back. It would truly, then, be for nothing that he was drifting out there in the darkness of the North Sea.

She wanted a lucky name for the baby, feeling he would need it. So it was natural she should turn to the great saint of Orkney, revered in the north at least as much for waging war on pirates as for piety. Magnus was a fighter and a miracle-worker, his tomb famous for cures. He should be able to protect a baby. She fell asleep on that thought.

In a couple of days she knew it wasn't typhus fever. Vaccination was not so widespread yet that the pustules of smallpox could be unfamiliar. Jamie came down with it, too. In both of them it ran its course, drying up and scarring, invading throats and lungs, bronchopneumonia turning to pleurisy so that neither was ever really in good health again. But it left them alive, so they were luckier than many.

Magnus, however, continued healthy and cheerful almost up to the moment when he developed a deep red haemorrhagic rash all over his body. What had started suddenly went on with violent swiftness: the baby named for the battling earl, the saint whose powers outlived his murder, was dead before he had so much as become infectious.

Chapter 10
Lerwick: 1842

The woman was taking two hands to carry the bucket of water, and even then she stopped and put it down every so often. She flexed her back, and looked round at the four-year-old dragging up the hill, some way behind her.

"Come on, Jamie, it's no' far noo." He seemed to make an effort for a few moments, but soon fell back to his old speed. He was thin and pale-faced, and looked to have a cold.

It was a long way to the well from their new room. After the smallpox, when she missed so much work, they had never had any chance of paying the rent at Martinmas. Maybe she could have persuaded Sinclair Goudie to give them longer, for he was genuinely sorry for her. But he was the owner's agent; he had to get the money eventually, and in an odd way his very kindness made her feel ill at ease: she hated owing money to him, more than to most people. So they had flitted again. At the moment, they owed money to a Mr Greig, and she saw no prospect of paying most of it. No doubt they would move on once more, come Martinmas.

She still had the same old energy; her hands still moved in and out of work as if of their own volition. But she was never as strong again as she had been before the smallpox. She had to rest more; there was a stitch in her left side when she walked, and she was soon out of breath. Most of the time she shrugged it off. Jamie's health worried her more; small and slight for his age, he seemed to catch everything going.

The Kirk had paid for Magnus to be buried; three and sixpence, the small coffin had cost. It had caused some administrative bother, because the parish didn't consider that she and Magnus had lived in Lerwick long enough to be their responsibility and had therefore claimed the money back from her home parish of Northmavine. But she didn't know that. He lay in the soil of Lerwick now, as his father lay offshore: she knew, objectively, that James' body might have drifted to Norway by now, but she could never look at the harbour without thinking of him there.

Jamie caught up, and she put her arm around his thin shoulders. He made no objection, but he didn't respond either. There was something odd about him, since the smallpox and Mansie's death. He had always been friendly, responsive to her affection and loving in his turn towards the baby. When James had died, he had been just old enough to notice he was gone, and to ask for Dada once or twice, but he had seemed to accept Kirstie's statement that his father wouldn't be coming back.

At first he had hardly noticed Mansie's death, being so ill himself at the time. Kirstie was in grief over the baby, far more so than made sense to the well-meaning churchfolk who pointed out to her that the Lord had done all for the best and relieved her of a burden she could not have hoped to manage. It was a while before she noticed how withdrawn Jamie was. He asked if Mansie would be coming back, but didn't seem surprised at the answer. Then he puzzled her by asking where James' loom was. It had stood in the corner of the room until he died; she had sold it for food before they flitted to new lodgings, much to the chagrin of the landlord, who reckoned he was owed it for back rent. Jamie had never mentioned it before. Over the next few days he asked about other things that had been sold, or neighbours from former lodgings.

It was as if he were beginning to expect the things and people in his life to be transient, to float in with the high tide and out again with the low. His mother, indeed, had been the only fixture, and he might have reacted by clinging to her the more, but he didn't: instead he seemed to loosen his hold on things, to stand back from his life. Although, facially, he resembled his father, there was a look in his eyes which made her think of Hercules.

The room where they lived now was in a little court that opened off one of the lanes. As they turned in, Kirstie became aware of a man leaning on a house door opposite. She had not seen him before: either he was new or he usually worked during the day. He was tall, with iron-grey hair and a grin which struck her as vaguely mocking. But he seemed sincere enough when he sauntered forward and spoke: "Ye're ower tired, lass." He gestured at the bucket. Kirstie began automatically to protest that she could manage, but he paid no heed; just took the bucket from her and started off up the steps. His back and shoulders were very muscular, she noticed.

For the first time in many months, she remembered how she had ached for the feel of James' body in bed, after he died. Even with her and Jamie in it, the bed had felt huge and empty; sometimes she woke from a dream that it was she, and not James, drifting in the night and the North Sea. But then a few months later the baby had come, and the sensual warmth of the small body nuzzling at hers had pushed the memories of a different kind of sensuality way back in her mind. And she had been ill: the only physical sensation she could recall feeling recently was tiredness. But now, following the tall man up the steps, she was mildly shocked to find herself wondering how his body felt in bed.

She put it quickly from her mind, and in fact they shared nothing that time but a cup of tea and a chat. But when he left, she thought a lot about him. His name was Jerome Caddel; like her he was country-born and had come to Lerwick looking for work. Until recently he had found plenty of it, at the labouring, which was why she hadn't seen him around, but now with times getting hard there was less to do. When he could, he earned well; he was a strong, energetic man — but not a young one. He was, in fact, fifty years old when he came into her life.

Before long, he was spending time in her room most days. When he was in work, he would come back there afterwards for his tea, like any husband. Sometimes he slept there; other nights he went back to his own room round the corner. Kirstie had never been to this room: he asked nobody back to it.

"Dat's me ain place," he said when she asked why.

"I cud redd[10] it up fir ye," she suggested.

"I dae fine by me sel. It's as clean noo as whin me wife wis alive."

Kirstie had not liked to ask how long he had been a widower. If he missed his wife, he gave very little sign of it. Though he did not object to Kirstie cooking and sewing for him, he could do it well enough for himself if he had to, as he occasionally reminded her. She got the impression that he had been surprised, and not ill-pleased, to find how well he could manage on his own. He was like an old bachelor in some ways, fussy and neat and handier about the house than most men. But he had never learned James' skill at fashioning toys, for he had no children.

He was amiable enough to Jamie, from a distance: in fact they virtually ignored each other. Caddel had forgotten how to talk to a child, while Jamie treated him like a casual acquaintance, who might or might not be around tomorrow. It seemed to suit the man quite well, better at any rate than Kirstie's occasional attempts to fuss over his food or clothes. It soon became plain that he was irritated by the suggestion that he needed any other person. Sometimes he would stay away, as if to prove the point; to protect the aloneness that had become a matter of pride for him.

But in one thing, of course, he could hardly deny he needed company. Kirstie for her part was happy to have him in her bed and made no secret of it. He dropped in for meals, stayed overnight, helped her with the rent money when he was in work: it was not surprising if the neighbours took him for a fixture. Some of them, at this point, began to refer to her as Kirstie Caddel. It might have been sarcasm, or moral disapproval, or maybe they did really take her for his wife — or even his daughter. At all events, she did not stop them, though she never used the name herself.

10 "redd" : clean.

Her body, so long tired and stiff, began to relax and feel at ease. A friend at the well joked that it was having a man in your bed that did it. Kirstie blushed and murmured that it was just the warm weather coming on.

It was a while before it occurred to her that there might be another reason for it. But she had borne two children already, and could not be in doubt for long.

She sat down with her knitting to think. Pale spring sun was striking through the window; there was not much strength in it yet, and outside, the sharp breeze would have made her feel cold, but she was warm in the shelter of the room. From the court below, children's voices rose, playing and quarrelling; in someone's backyard, a pig grunted. She closed her eyes, and let the sun warm the lids.

Financially, of course, it was plain bad news. She still had trouble getting the rent together, and would have found it hard to clothe Jamie without the help of people like Margaret Angus. In a few years he would be old enough to go to the school, which she wanted very much for him. She herself, like most country girls of her generation, had scraped a minimum of education in the few years before she became old enough to help out on the croft; she could read, with difficulty, but writing was beyond her. James had been a bit better off, but not much. One of the things he had wanted in Lerwick was to give his son a better start than his own had been, so that he didn't necessarily have to do just what his father had done all his life.

Besides, if Jamie was at the school, she could get work outside the home, which would pay better than the eternal knitting and spinning — maybe, at last, they could get ahead of the game. It really was no time to saddle herself with a helpless new baby.

Then there was Caddel. She was not at all sure how he would react: if he refused to take any responsibility and walked out on them, they would be in trouble. Caring for two infants on her own had been hard enough the last time, and if anything, times were worse now.

She leaned back in the sun, her knitting forgotten, and smiled with pure pleasure. Whatever she tried to tell herself, she knew she was happy about the baby. She liked having something to cuddle; she always had. She told Jamie, hoping he would share her happiness, but he seemed no more than politely interested. She tried to convince him: "It'll be like Mansie come back again." But he looked unconvinced.

She took much longer to tell Caddel. In fact it was he, one day, who asked curiously what she had to look so pleased about. (He was finding work hard to come by; the growing rumours about Hay & Ogilvy were making other employers nervous). So she told him. He paused, laughed shortly and said he still didn't see what there was to be pleased about.

"I laek bairns", said Kirstie mildly.

"Aye, weel, ye're welcome.". He turned back to his food.

Kirstie had never supposed he would be instantly delighted, and let the subject drop for the time. He picked at his dinner for a while, then burst out: "I'm no' mairryin' ye, lass, dat's shure".

"Ye wir mairrit ance," Kirstie said timidly, "wir ye no' happy?"

"Aye, I wis weel enyoch. An' I'm weel noo. I laek fine bein' by mesel'"

Over the next few days, it became plain that he was not going to change his mind. Kirstie tried at first to get him interested in the idea of a child of his own, but he was like an animal which has sensed a trap. He liked her where she was, on the outside of his life where he could visit her now and then, but he wanted nothing near the core of him; nothing which would force him to change his rooted habits; above all, no responsibilities. He could tolerate Jamie, because he felt the lad's welfare was none of his business, but he reacted with angry resentment to the notion of a being in the world for whom he would be responsible. Though she had often heard some woman at the well complain, half-seriously, that another baby would ruin her, Kirstie had never come across anyone who literally didn't want any children, ever, and she could not think how to argue with him. When she began to look obviously pregnant, he became uncomfortable even being with her and soon left off visiting the room.

The last time they were really together was when they went to the Kirk to be admonished for fornication. This was more or less unavoidable; to defy the Church's censure would have invited more social disapproval than the sin which had caused it. But Kirstie was very scared. Both in the north and in Lerwick, she had often enough sat in the congregation and watched some conspicuous unfortunate shifting from foot to foot under the fiery rebuke from the pulpit. She had wondered how she would feel in that situation, as people do who never expect to be there.

In the event, she remembered very little about it. When she first stood up, she felt the blood rush to her face; she went hot and cold by turns and something seemed to happen to her sight and hearing; there were suddenly an impossible number of people in the church, the sea of faces blurred, and the minister's voice was lost in a noise like an ocean, roaring and ebbing in her ears. She heard almost nothing of what he said. Once, his voice reached her, when he was picturing the sin of lechery with what seemed rather indecent fervour, and gave himself a fit of coughing.

Caddel, beside her, took advantage of the moment to wink. "He's got an awfu' lewd imagination", he whispered, and grinned. He was much more at ease than she; he cared very little what the minister said, or the congregation thought, as long as they recognised this curious little ceremony as his certificate of bachelorhood — guilty of fornication he might be, but at least no-one any more would suppose he was married.

Kirstie managed a faint smile, and felt buoyed up a little. He had always had nerve, and that wryness about him; it was one of the things she had liked. The child inside her fluttered and she put her hands over it, as if to screen it from the disapproving eyes below.

Chapter 11
Lerwick: 1843

It was Saturday morning, which meant the houses of the well-to-do each had a patient queue of beggars waiting outside. Not only were there more of them than formerly, they were often a different kind: decent-looking folk, craftsmen maybe or small shopkeepers, you might guess; women in clothes which were clean but patched almost beyond recognising, and old folk, who had obviously never begged before, in a misery of shame.

Hay & Ogilvy's great enterprise at Freefield had finally gone bankrupt, and the crash had sent its ripples right out to the edge of its small world, as Charles Ogilvy had feared. The coopers, dockers, labourers, who had been thrown out of work had wives, children and parents depending on them; the shopkeepers missed the trade of those who could no longer afford to buy as they did before, and the wives trying to make up for their husbands' wages could not get a decent price for their knitting and spinning from the shopkeepers. All in all, the Royal Commission inquiring into the need for a reform of the poor law had chosen an interesting year to visit Shetland.

There were those, in Shetland and elsewhere, who felt strongly that it was wrong to think of institutionalising charity, putting a legal obligation on people to give through the rates, rather than leaving it to their conscience at the church door. (And creating, too, a legal right to relief for those who had always received it as a favour: where would that end?) But the plain facts were that the need was greater than private charity was able or willing to meet. At least, so it seemed; in truth nobody was sure of the real scale of the problem, which was why the Commissioners were on their travels.

They were intrigued by the fact that there was a semi-official begging day. "It's a convenience, really," William Hay pointed out, "it means we're only troubled with it the one day."

"Some do come other days," put in Gilbert Duncan in his gentle voice, "the better sort that aren't used with begging yet, and like to think it'll no' be for long."

"I suppose there will be a great deal of spirits drunk among the labouring classes", observed a hatchet-faced individual on the Commission.

"Och, no, I wudna say just exactly that. They take it when they can get it, ye ken, but they've no' the means to drink heavy."

The Commissioners had come armed with a set of questions. Some were genuinely designed to elicit information, about average wages and rents, for instance, but some, like the drink question, they thought they knew the answers to already: everyone knew the poor drank too much.

"It's no' men out o' work that drink to excess," remarked Sheriff Duncan, testily, "and since William's misfortune," — he nodded at Hay, leaning back in his chair, at ease with a cigar — "there's many that canna get the work to support themselves and their families. That's where the half of the poverty comes from. And the rest is because everyone that fails in the country comes to Lerwick."

"And because no' everyone gives as they should," Gilbert put in. "We've too many poor, and too little money to share amang them, aye, but there cud be more, if there werena folk well off that give nothing. It's an awful thing, that we do need an assessment and a rate set, because folk winna give enough at the Kirk door."

His brother nodded vigorously, but William Hay demurred.

"Ye're talkin' about a drop in the ocean, Gilbert; if there was ever a proper assessment of folk in need of relief in this town, it'd be beyond the ratepayers to fund it. If it was just the poor old sick folk, maybe, but ye'd have to draw the regulations to keep out the able-bodied, work or no work."

"Would you want an assessment that included the able-bodied?" one of the Commissioners asked Sheriff Duncan.

"No," he said heavily, "it's no' their fault they've no work, but I wudna want that. William's right, for one thing, the town cudna pay it, but anyway ... it canna be right for a young hearty man to get to seeing himself as a pauper; as someone that canna pay his way and care for his bairns, but has to be aye helped, like the old bodies."

Gilbert nodded, and said softly: "It doesna tak' long on the poor roll, before ye see they've no hope of bettering themselves. It's degrading at first, and then it gets to be a habit; there's a way of being a pauper in spirit."

One of the Commissioners hinted delicately that he had heard it said Shetlanders tended to be apathetic.

"They've no security of tenure, no work in winter; in the country the lairds have them aye in debt; even in town here the rents are so high, they canna help but fall behind in a bad season ...." The Sheriff was getting somewhat heated. "Aye, maybe they feel they canna alter things much. But they wad work willingly, if there was work to be had; ask the

Navy. If the Government wad pay to make work, building roads or whatever, it'd maybe cost no more than assessing folk for poor relief, and they cud keep their pride, forbye."

"I fear such — ah — radical solutions lie outside our terms of reference. If we might now pass on to such matters as diet and housing...?" And this was the signal for Dr Cowie to mount his hobby-horse about how tea-drinking debilitated the poor. Even he, though, blamed much of the town's disease on the miserable state of the housing, while the Duncan brothers nodded assent. William Hay stayed out of that one. He had owned quite a bit of the town's housing, until lately, and still hoped to again. And he reckoned if you gave that class of person palaces, they would still make hovels out of them. But you could never convince folk like Gilbert of that, any more than you could convince Charles Ogilvy that it wasn't his fault so many were out of work. There were folk, in William's view, who had an exaggerated idea of what they owed their neighbour, and of how much they could do to help him. In the end, there was just yourself.

In one of the long lines of Saturday beggars, outside the Sievwrights' place in Sheriff's Closs, stood Kirstie and Jamie. He was five now, thin and slight but still growing faster than she could keep him in clothes and shoes. The Sievwrights had young children, and would sometimes give her outgrown things for him.

From time to time, he got bored and wandered off to play in the puddles. She called him back sometimes, but she did not watch him as narrowly as she might once have done, either because he was older or because she was occupied with the small baby huddled close in her shawl. She cooed and talked to it a lot, rubbing noses with it and stroking its sparse dark hair, though it was really too young to notice much.

Jamie himself had no interest in it. His pessimism at Kirstie's suggestion that it might be Mansie come back had proved well-founded: once he heard it was a girl, he took no further notice, except to resent the amount of his mother's time it took. Kirstie on the other hand was wrapped up in the baby.

She felt it had nobody but her. Caddel had been in no way softened by the actual birth of his child; he still wanted nothing to do with her. When he passed Kirstie in the street these days, they did not so much as give each other good morning, though sometimes he would glance at the bundle in the shawl with more resentment than Jamie did. He refused absolutely to support her with money; yet, awkward as this was, it seemed less to Kirstie than his refusal to feel anything.

Neither were he and Jamie the only ones who had hard looks for the little thing. Times were terrible, since the Freefield crash; there was no work, and no decent market for the knitting and spinning. But for all that, she probably would not have been standing with the Saturday beggars, if it had not been for the baby. Even when she was ill after Magnus, she had never begged before, because she'd never had to; there had always been folk who were sorry for her and would help her out now and again. It was different now. She could see well enough the disapproval in the faces of ladies, like Margaret Angus, who had liked the idea of a widow caring for her late husband's child, but felt much less kindly towards the same woman caring for an illegitimate baby.

Her own kind, the poor women from the lanes, were far more sympathetic, knowing it might have been them. The child began to mew with hunger, and she had to feed it discreetly, under the shawl. Grizel Cogle, next to her in the line of beggars, grimaced understandingly.

"Du wis unlucky dere, richt enyoch. It's no' fair dat weemin's left wid a' da trouble."

Kirstie stroked the baby's hair again. Everyone she knew assumed it had come as a burden to her, or that she should be ashamed of it; there seemed no welcome in the world for it, unless from her. She felt an intense, protective warmth towards it, which deepened with every pursed mouth or friendly commiseration she encountered.

Perhaps that was why she had given it her own name. Or perhaps because, like Magnus, this baby would need a fighter's name, and she didn't trust saints any more. And perhaps also because, physically as well as financially, the child had nothing of her father. She was already the image of Kirstie.

The long wait proved worthwhile; they gave her some shoes for Jamie. She hurried home, hoping to get some more spinning done if the baby would leave her in peace. With the low price the merchants were paying these days, you had to do more and more just to buy tatties and a twist of tea. They hadn't had fish, even, for some time. She was behind with the rent, again.

The Commissioners finished their deliberations for the morning. The secretary began to sort out the notes he would write up later: trades, wages, rents; the doctors on hygiene and diet: *potatoes, fish. milk. a little meal; no meat*, the minister: *on a Saturday there are never less than thirty people begging at my door*. One of his colleagues called to him to leave that for now and come to lunch, and he put down his pen with alacrity. William Hay was taking them home to lunch, and they'd been his guests before. After a morning's work, it was pleasant to look forward to relaxing in the graciously furnished house, with William's imported food and wine. Hay led them off down one of the lanes, to where his gig was waiting; they picked their way gingerly past the middens, wondering how he could stride ahead so unconcernedly.

Kirstie, emerging from her room to empty the bucket, saw the cheerful, florid man go by, laughing and talking, and shook her head uncomprehendingly. She knew who he was, and how he'd failed in business: her room was in one of the houses he had once owned, before the estate was sequestrated to pay the creditors. The house agent had explained "bankrupt" to her.

"It means he canna pay his way."

Having been so often in that position herself, she felt quite sorry for him. But the next time she saw him in the Street, he was coming out of the hotel, as well-dressed as ever, looking at his ease, not hopeless nor ill-fed, nor like a man who sees himself without the rent money next Martinmas. She was baffled: she had seen plenty of people who couldn't pay their way, but he resembled none of them. How could he look so tranquil, and him with a large family? She thought of the coopers and carpenters whose jobs had gone with Freefield, desperate now for labouring work, or a place on a fishing boat, or anything they could get, those who hadn't already given up and joined the Saturday queues. And the wives, finding no market for their spinning, looking round the house and wondering what furniture to sell, trying to stop their men from sinking into apathy or spending what little there was on drink.

Later, someone did try to explain to her how people like Hay could fail, and yet still live much as before. But she never really understood it.

Chapter 12
Lerwick: 1844

A year after the Hay & Ogilvy crash, the partners had reacted to it each in his own typical way. William Hay was setting up Hay & Co, and Charles Ogilvy was dead, at the age of forty-two.

Nobody much doubted that the bankruptcy had killed him. He had lost no more than Hay had: ships, works, houses and the rents on them, but Hay had never made the error of investing his dreams in Freefield along with his money. He had lost his means of business, and would have to find another: it was inconvenient, but no more. Since he was convinced he could do it all again, he did not feel that he personally was a failure.

Charles Ogilvy, on the other hand, could not see a shop boarded up or a cooper out of work without feeling he was to blame for it. He had "failed", in the phrase of his time, which did not distinguish between business and personal failure. Neither, deep down, did he. He had had a vision of his town's future as he wanted it to be; when he contemplated what it now looked like being, something in him chose to shut down rather than see it. The town council showed him the honour he no longer felt himself entitled to; they had the town bell tolled and Samuel Henry issued a proclamation ordering the shops closed for his funeral. Not, as some of the shopkeepers observed, that it was much of a sacrifice to be interrupted in selling what no-one could afford to buy.

Maybe Charles Ogilvy had passed on his brooding anxiety to his family, for his brother-in-law Gilbert Duncan died the same year at fifty-seven; no great age for a Shetlander. Charles Gilbert, his eldest, was twenty-eight when he found himself responsible for his mother and his nine brothers and sisters. So he had little time for angling, now.

He had set up as a lawyer, a writer as they called it, since law seemed to have become the Duncan family business. His office was only just across the Street from his cousin Andrew's; handy, as Andrew had remarked, if the lad wanted to drop in for advice. Actually it was Andrew, more often, whose head would appear round Charles Gilbert's door, inquiring: "Have ye time for a crack?" He would sit on the edge of the desk, scattering pipe ash over the papers, and generally impede whatever work his young cousin had on hand. Nevertheless, Charles

Gilbert was grateful. Despite the warmth and closeness of his immediate family, he was feeling a great gap where his father and his uncle Charles Ogilvy had been.

It was more than the want of their personal presence, though nearly every day he would find himself missing something small and characteristic, like the way Ogilvy, with one of his foreign guests, would switch from one language to another without thinking about it; or his father's gentle way of indicating total disagreement: "Och, I wudna say just exactly that ..." All his life, they had been the models of his future; it had been accepted that one day he would be on the town council, like Gilbert, or chief magistrate, like Charles. Probably, he still would; only now there was no-one to be like, no picture of himself twenty or thirty years hence. His family already looked to him for guidance: he felt he had been pitchforked into being for others the kind of figure he still needed in his own life.

At such a time, Andrew was a sympathetic presence to find perched on his desk, even if he too had his worries. In fact the future looked emptier to him, by a long way, than it did to his young cousin. Charles Ogilvy had actually been Andrew's junior by two years; the death had come as a small shock of mortality. Even worse, Uncle Gilbert had been eleven years younger than Andrew's father the Sheriff (he was retired now, but nobody could get used to thinking of him as anything else.) The old man was shaken by the loss of the brother he had never thought to outlive, and by the worsening problems of the town; his vigour and optimism were failing and for the first time he looked like someone who might not have much longer. Andrew's attempts to reassure him were unavailing, mainly because he was as unhappy about it as his father.

They were a close, affectionate family: Andrew could see himself, before long, in the same position young Charles Gilbert was in now, physically aching to touch someone who would never be in reach again. But there was more; once his father had gone, he could never think of himself as the younger generation again. At least, for Charles Gilbert, the question was still what he would do with his life. For himself it was what he had, and still more had not done: what now he would never do.

On Commercial Street the wind was raw; he hunched into his overcoat as he passed one of the seaward lanes. It was October; a sunny day, but the sun seemed pale and remote, giving little warmth. The Street had an ill-cared-for look; people had other uses for their cash, this year, than refurbishing house and shop fronts. Here and there, despite the cold, small groups of men loitered: out of work, he supposed, and tired of being under their wives' feet. Or maybe it was the wives who were tired. Passing Robertson's shop, he heard raised voices: a couple of women arguing with the shopkeeper about the value of the stockings they had brought him. He was protesting that he had to sell them on, and where was the demand with no cash about; aye, it might well be true that the Queen liked them, but he could hardly send them all to London; anyway, he supposed the poor body could only wear one pair at a time like everyone else. One of the women was quite elderly. She had a couple of grandchildren with her, and kept repeating: "Whaur'll we find da rent?" She sounded desperate; of course, Martinmas was coming close. He wondered whether the children's parents were still living, or did they have only the grandmother to provide for them. There were so many like her, now; it was depressing even to think about it. Andrew found himself fighting a desire to feed and clothe them on Saturday and put them out of his mind for the rest of the week.

He huddled deeper into his coat. He was bound for the courtroom in Fort Charlotte, wanting to consult the Procurator Fiscal about a matter he had on hand. The mere thought of the Fiscal made him feel old again; Archibald Greig was only twenty-six, a ridiculous age really, but he had more or less inherited the job from his father. At this rate, Andrew thought morosely, he would soon be consulting men young enough to be his grandsons.

In the Fort, Greig was at work, and Andrew sat down to wait in the courtroom, half-listening to the cases. The drone of the sheriff's clerk sent his mind drifting; the high windows overlooked the sea, and outside, gulls were wheeling and balancing in the wind. Sometimes they would all dive down together in a raucous frenzy, and he knew some fishing-boat must have thrown rubbish overboard. Like an accompaniment to the screaming birds, he heard vaguely in the background the well-known formalities of an indictment.

.... that on the 8th of October 1844 the said Christina Inkster or Jamieson[11] did wickedly and feloniously steal and thieftuously away take a child's cotton frock ....

Andrew Duncan came jarringly awake. The sudden, incongruous object of the sonorous legal phrases caused him to feel he had never really heard them before. He looked for the first time at the criminal. She would be about thirty: thin, dark-haired, dark-eyed. Her clothes were clean, but very worn. She looked not so much scared as bewildered, like someone who was where she had never expected to be.

The conventional words of the indictment rolled on: a few other wicked and felonious thefts were mentioned, a child's bedgown and a small cotton shift. She nodded when they were named; in admission of guilt, or possibly because they were the only words she understood. It was established that her brief career of crime (it seemed to have begun and ended on the night of the 8th) had taken in the washing-lines of various Lerwick backyards — including, Andrew noted wryly, one

11 "Inkster or Jamieson" : Women were often still known by their maiden as well as their married names (as happens in those Nordic countries where patronymics are used).

belonging to a Sheriff Officer: she didn't seem to have been very adept at it.

She agreed that she understood the charge, and admitted it. Then she was asked if she had anything to say. This seemed to surprise her, almost to take her aback. Andrew Duncan found himself willing her to answer. He wanted her to tell the court how it came about that she had to steal clothes for her child; he wanted to know himself. But after a pause, she shook her head.

The sentence was one month, and as she was escorted out, she passed close to Andrew. Her face was sallow, he saw, and pockmarked; older than it should have been. He said impulsively: "You should have spoken for yourself; they'd maybe have listened." Her eyes widened slightly. In the aging face, they looked young, and oddly peaceful. She said mildly: "Whit wid I say? I took da tings."

Afterwards he asked Archibald Greig what would happen to her child. The young man ran a hand through his hair and said worriedly: "There's two bairns, I've had to put them out with a woman and Gude kens what she'll charge for a month. More than the clothes cost, that's sure."

"Have they a father living?"

"One of them has, but he's no' awful concerned. I'll have to see if I can't dun him for the money, though."

"How did she come so ill off?"

"Och, she lost her husband a few years since, at the fishing I think, and they've just gone down and down, the way these folk do. And of course they're no help to themselves; there's her goes and has a bairn to another man, when she can't feed the first one and pay her rent ... Strangely enough, it seems I was her landlord once; I'd no recollection of it until I looked at the papers of the case, but she lived in a house of mine two years back. The rent was short, of course: two quarters she was there, at ten shillings the quarter, and I only saw seven-and-six of it."

"Did ye go to law?"

"No, what for? She cudna pay; if they'd put her in the jail I'd have seen no more of my money. Ye're gey curious the day, Andrew."

It was only some time after leaving the Fort that Andrew realised he had never mentioned the matter on which he came to see Greig . The case still ran in his head: Latinate phrases and baby clothes, *thieftuously and feloniously*, Greig's missing rent and the woman's passive, marked face. He did not return to his office. It was getting late in the day; those who had work were beginning to come from it. He saw a little line of women dragging themselves up to the Street from the fish-gutting. Some had bleeding hands, but they seemed not to notice. They walked stiffly, like people with backache, not speaking, their faces expressionless with tiredness. He looked into eyes that must be as dead and staring as the fishy ones in the barrels.

Everything he saw seemed to strike him more sharply and painfully than usual. The begging children by the shop doorways; the drunken man slumped in the shadows — at most times Andrew would have felt nothing but impatience with him, but now he had a curiosity to know what the man was like sober, and what had made him get himself into that state. Intemperance and profligacy, as Sam Henry would say .... With no real idea where he was going, he came to the harbour.

A late fishing-boat was tying up, the men working in the same tired, mechanical silence that he had observed in the fish-gutters. They didn't look to have caught much. As he watched them, one glanced up and met his gaze: a big bearded man with black eyes that might sometimes have been merry, when all the life and light hadn't been emptied out of them. He looked as if nothing had gone right for him all day.

Andrew found himself wondering what the man would do that night. Maybe he'd have a drink, if he had the price on him. Maybe it would turn into two or three, however many it took to drown the memory of the day. Then next week he'd be short of the rent, and someone like Sam Henry would tell him how improvident he was.

Or maybe he'd find a woman. Someone who needed the money and would be the vessel where he could pour all the frustration and tension and failure knotted up in him. Or someone who needed him; maybe he was going home to one of those dead-eyed women from the gutting sheds. Her cut hands and his rope-calloused ones, trying to strike a spark from each other's bodies before exhaustion claimed them. There must be a great tide of coming together in this town at night, Andrew mused; for love, for money, out of boredom or bitterness, but most of all for comfort, to keep company against the dark and unwind from such a day in the only way they knew.

The fisherman stepped heavily on to the quayside and set off up the lane. Drained of strength as it was, his big body looked incongruously helpless. How little his strength could actually do. It could help him catch the herring if they came, but it couldn't bring them if they didn't. It could keep him from starving, but never make him so much money that he need not worry about the future. It made him able to hold a woman and make children with her, but not to free her from all those hours at the fish-gutting. The man stumbled against a cobble, which he could hardly lift his foot to clear. Andrew felt his heart go out to him. He hoped he would find a woman, that they would all find someone, all the seamen and the fish-gutters, labourers and skivvies, widows and whores, those who needed the money and those who needed someone to shelter in for a while.

The man turned a corner and was gone, but the surge of tenderness, like a physical ache, in Andrew involved the whole town now, and the North Sea, and the red star at Orion's shoulder, and the ugly fish, of whatever misshapen and unsaleable breed, which had been caught in the herring nets and lay so still now on the quayside. He felt restless, wanting to translate his feelings into some kind of action, but none seemed enough.

PART FOUR

FEELINGS OF PRIDE

Chapter 13
Lerwick: 1845

"We could call it Fox Lane."

"Aye, maybe ... but we'd have to make a Pitt Lane as well, to be fair to the Tories. What would we use for that?"

Archibald Greig ran his finger along a map, and looked up: "Joseph Leask's Closs."

Andrew Duncan leaned back in his chair and drained the last drops from a glass. "Aye, that 'll do. Would ye pass the bottle, Thomas?"

The Police Commission's sub-committee for the re-naming of Lerwick's lanes was in session in Andrew's study: they were only five and it seemed logical to combine business with pleasure. Andrew had never been so much a committee man as his father and uncle, but he loved this one. Most of the leading townsmen were thinking about the Parochial Board which would have to be set up now the new Poor Law Act had gone through; all the talk was of whether relief should be confined to the old and sick; how the poor could be stopped from flooding in from the country; above all what poor rate would be set and who would be liable. He liked to escape from it, to something that felt frivolous by contrast.

It was necessary, though, as he sometimes pointed out to Charles Gilbert when that serious young man raised a sardonic eyebrow about the amount of time he spent on it. Because the town had grown in such a haphazard way, the lanes were mostly named after whoever had happened to build them, or had an unusual-looking house there, or a particular job. Over the years, many names had ceased to be appropriate and been replaced, or semi-replaced, with new ones on the same principle, so that persons of different generations were sometimes in doubt as to whether they were speaking of the same place. The idea was to find names which would honour the town's traditions, but would not become irrelevant as soon as someone died, or some business moved away.

"What'll we call South Kirk Closs?" asked Greig. "After all, there's no kirk there now, just the Subscription Rooms."

They bandied this one around for a while. It was true the building was no longer a church; on the other hand it was where the town's first church had long stood. In the end they renamed it Church Lane. (It had been decided at the outset that closses sounded too old-fashioned and rustic, though Andrew had some secret regrets for them.)

They renamed most of those lanes that were named for individuals, even Sheriff's Closs. This was the one they were in, named for former Sheriff Duncan, Andrew's father, who had built his house and Andrew's there; and the other members of the committee offered to let the name stand, in view of his eminence. Andrew might have been tempted, had he not known his father wouldn't approve.

"It's full of lawyers," he observed, "call it Law Lane." The old man would like that, he thought; to have the law honoured through him, as it were.

One of the few times they broke their rule was when Gilbert Tait, studying the map, called out: "Burns Closs". Andrew grimaced, and someone facetiously suggested Fever Lane.

"It's a filthy place, right enough," admitted Greig, his nose wrinkling fastidiously, "a body would think old Magnus would take shame to own it, let alone call it for himself."

"He's fine and proud of it, as long as folk pay him rent to live there," said Andrew. He got up abruptly and walked about the room a while; then turned and grinned. "Dunna change it at all; leave his name on it."

"But the idea was *not* to leave them named for private persons, as if we wanted to immortalise ourselves," Greig objected.

"Aye, Archie, but this one's different; can ye think of a more fitting way to immortalise the old leech?"

"Burns Lane, then. No closses. Talking of rents, I hear William Hay's buying houses again. It didna take him long to climb back. It's a black shame poor Charles Ogilvy let that crash worry him into his grave; he could have seen Freefield working again, if he'd held on like William."

"He was ower worried about the folk that wouldna be fit to climb back. They're no' all as enterprising as William, and they didn't all think to have wealthy relatives. Even if the work at Freefield gets back to what it was, there'll be a fine sight of folk that never do."

"You should be setting up the Parochial Board, Andrew, not renaming the lanes."

"God, no, it's depressing enough just to think about the way things are, leave alone trying to mend matters. Charles Gilbert's welcome to that."

It had been raining for weeks, with a hard, driving wind, but overnight the rain had turned to big, loose flakes of snow. After the noise of the rain rapping at windows and splashing on the stones, the snow was awesomely quiet. It fell steadily, patiently, filling up crevices, blurring the outlines of things. The ponies' feet made no sound in it; no birds sang; even the wind was smothered.

Whenever there was a brief break in the fall, children appeared in the lanes. The older lads had makeshift sleds; the few people who ventured out in the Street in such weather were in constant danger of being hit by some contraption of driftwood or orange-boxes hurtling at speed out of the steep lanes that seemed to be designed for such sport.

From time to time, the mothers appeared at their doors to check up on them, and chat across to each other. Kirstie hugged a thin shawl about her. In her girlhood, and even up to a few years ago, the cold would not have worried her, but these days she never seemed to be able to get warm. Since the year '41, when she had the smallpox, her breath came harder; sometimes when she tried to breathe deeply, she felt as if her left lung were stuck to something and would tear if she breathed too hard.

Jamie often seemed to be short of breath too; he was sledging with the others but stopping to cough a lot. The little girl, not yet three, watched the older ones, wide-eyed, clasping a piece of old blanket around her shoulders in imitation of her mother. An elderly woman, across the way, looked at her and smiled.

"Eh, da peerie ean's da livin' laekness o' dee, Kirstie, she's got naethin' o' her fadir."

The child, hearing itself spoken of, glanced up as the mother looked down fondly at it, and the two pairs of dark eyes reflected each other perfectly.

"Aye," said Kirstie with feeling, "naethin's richt; he'll no' pay a penny ta feed her or buy claes ta her."

The old woman clucked sympathetically. "Maybe, whin dey mak' da new poor roll, things'll be easier." She was hoping so, for her own sake; it was hard to find the rent on the amount of work a fifty-seven-year-old widow could do.

"Why wid dey be?" asked Kirstie sceptically, "da kirk aye had a poor roll, an' ye cudna get help fra it aless ye were dead or deein'."

"Aye, but da new board 'll have mair money. Da kirk just had whit folk gae at da door." That was Laurina Laurenson, glancing up from her knitting. Laurie belonged with the women, not the sledging children; she was thirteen now and had been working for a living as long as she remembered.

"Whit money's da board got, den?"

"Da rates." Though Laurie could not read or write, she knew most of what was going on, especially when it had to do with money; she had a child's sharp curiosity, directed almost entirely to adult concerns. "It's da law, folk hae ta gie it ta da board, an' dey gie it oot. I tink it's folk dat pay twa pund or mair in rent, day 'll aa hae ta pay. Dey're no' weel plaesed, Alex says."

Kirstie felt a queer pang of memory: when she and James first came to Lerwick, they must have been paying about that. If things had gone differently, maybe they'd have been respectable ratepayers now, complaining about the burden. Last time she had asked the kirk for help, they had offered to start a collection to send her back north.

She got news from her old home sometimes: there were still plenty of country folk flocking to town. Robert had children now (he had called his second child Christina, but she didn't know that). He and his family had a tiny croft, and his old mother to support into the bargain. Mary was married, too. Kirstie could think of nothing which would be less welcome to Robert, or to her sisters' husbands, than the sudden arrival of a family of extra dependants.

She thought about the quarter-wives. In her childhood she had seen so many of them: little old women tucked into the corners of croft rooms. They were widows, too old and weak to keep a farm going, who had no children to support them. The parish provided for them in an equitable fashion, sharing out the burden between all the households. One family would have such a woman for three months, then she would move on, with whatever bits of belongings she had, to the next, and so every quarter until she had been the rounds and it was the first household's turn again.

They were so quiet, like little mice, at their knitting, so deferential and grateful, always conscious of their place. Most families were kind to them, and they might get attached, perhaps, to a baby they minded or a child they sang to. But what was the use of that, when they must always move on? In hard times, when food was scarce, you could see them embarrassed by every mouthful they ate. They seemed to shrink and shrivel, as if trying to take up as little space as possible.

The anonymous board, by contrast, handing out money collected from you would never know whom, might be intimidating enough, but at least you wouldn't have to feel constantly grateful to it. If there was one thing most poor people, even those less sharp than Laurie, had grasped about the new Act, it was that the law, not charity, was at the back of it; that the money handed out to the poor would be something they had a legal right to. They clung to the idea, because it promised some dignity, not to mention more security than voluntary contributions which could dry up at any time.

Margaret Anderson, the old widow, was hoping for the rent money she could not earn. Ann Goodlad, with the disabled husband in Greenwich Hospital, had a sickly eight-year-old. Laurie fancied some furniture: all she and her brothers had in the room was the bed the three slept in. Kirstie wanted the means of sending her children to school, so that they wouldn't end up like Laurie. They were very modest wishes really; the lanes were full of small wishes like that.

That, of course, was the trouble, as the newly formed Parochial Board well knew. It was the sheer volume of small wishes that they were going to have difficulty in coping with.

The usual crowd were met to set it up; the little, closed society of property-owners who already met on the town council, and the Police Commission. Most of them were merchants: William Hay's brother was there; old Magnus Burns had sent his son David as proxy to oppose any hare-brained schemes for spending the heritors' money. There were doctors too, and lawyers: the Greigs, father and son, and Charles Gilbert Duncan, who also felt he was acting as a proxy for his father.

It quickly became apparent that they could do nothing much, yet. They needed to compile two lists: one of those legally entitled to relief, and another of those liable for rates. And then fix the rates, and the amounts of relief ... They set up a couple of committees, and elected some officers. Samuel Henry volunteered his services as clerk, and James Greig, young Archibald the Fiscal's father, as chairman. And they needed an Inspector of Poor, to give out the relief, or refuse it. There was even a contested election for that. Charles Gilbert was amazed anyone fancied being the man who'd have to say no to so many. In the end, David Burns was appointed, which Charles suspected was better news for the ratepayers than it was for the paupers. Magnus would be delighted, that was sure.

Chatting afterwards, Charles Gilbert remarked to Samuel Henry: "I'm surprised you'd volunteer for Clerk; you must have a weary enough time of it keeping the council's papers, without the board's as well"

"Well, well," Henry said affably, "it's no' everybody can't stand writing minutes. I like it fine; it's a pleasure to me to keep things in order. Forbye, I'm like yoursel': I think it's the duty of folk like us to be active on this Board." Charles Gilbert nodded, slightly surprised. "Aye," Henry continued, "there'll be sharp eyes needed, if the ratepayers' money isna to be thrown away on the undeserving." His face clouded over. "Here's Yule nearly upon us again, and ye ken fine what they'll be at, drinking and wasting good money in tar and gunpowder to watch it go up in smoke ... where's the thrift or reason in that? I tell you, I would die a happy man if I could put a stop to it."

"It's ower violent some years," Charles Gilbert admitted, "and I'm aye feared for the office window. But it's a bonny sight, all that brightness in the dark time of winter, and I don't see ye'll ever get the lads to give it up. Let's hope they have a quiet year." Henry snorted in disbelief.

Surveying the wreck of his office window, a few days later, Charles Gilbert had to admit that Henry's pessimism had been justified. It was seven in the morning, the dark just beginning to be streaked with blue and grey. The Street glittered with broken glass; on the rocks below the old Tolbooth, a thin spiral of smoke rose lazily from the last of the barrels, almost burnt out. One of the Sheriff Officers was trying keys in the Tolbooth door. All the special constables were inside, locked in at an earlier hour by the barrellers, who'd then thrown away the key. As he watched, the door was finally opened and they emerged, with a sheepish air, into the grey morning where the reek of gunpowder still lingered. On the light wind, ash drifted; the whole town made him think of an unswept hearth in the early hours, before the maid comes down. The only trace of last night's fire was in Henry's face: he was incandescent with anger.

Chapter 14
Lerwick: 1846

They were a strange pair at the desk, the young Sheriff Officer, neatly dressed, his brow furrowed as he pored over the form; and the woman, her clothes holed, smelling damp, looking as if they had been slept in for some time; her face lined and hollow-cheeked, but the eyes still clear and peaceful. He could not have put an age to her; when he asked her, in order to fill in the relevant space on the form, and she said thirty-three, he would have been equally unsurprised had she been ten years older.

He scanned the next question, raised an eyebrow and muttered: "Now whatever is that to do with anything? God, they ask some daft questions. What was your husband's father's name and trade, Mrs Jamieson?"

"James Peterson[12], fisherman," she said softly, and he wrote it down. She watched his quick fingers admiringly; it was a mystery to her how writing could come so easily to anyone's hands, as if it were something as natural as knitting. She could hardly read the long, complex form, never mind answer it. It was the application form for poor relief, and it was designed to ensure the Board's money was not wasted. It occurred to Peter Williamson, as he went on down the list, that it might also have been designed to deter prospective applicants from bothering.

It demanded, more or less, a potted biography: where you were born, who your parents and parents-in-law were, what they did, why you had come to Lerwick. Had you any trade or skill, any source of income from family, charity, savings: anywhere else, in short, to go but the Board? It added up to an overwhelming document: people like Peter were spending a lot of time filling them in for people like Kirstie.

Most of the time, he got the information he needed from her and then used his own clerkly phrases, as when, detailing what marketable skills she had learned at home, he translated "spinning and knitting" into "the common avocations of a Zetland girl". But when she answered the question: "have you ever lived by begging?", he wrote her words

12 "James Peterson" : Regular surnames were taking over from the Norse patronymics by this time. James the son of Peter named his son after himself, so we cannot tell if James Jamieson considered his second name a surname or patronymic.

down straight: *I have had to beg for my children, or they could not have been alive.*

The little one was on her mother's lap; dark-haired and dark-eyed, a smaller version of the mother, but somewhat better clothed and, by the look of it, fed. Peter glanced across at the boy, leaning against the far wall waiting, not looking about him or trying to invent a game out of his surroundings, just waiting. According to the form, he was eight, but he looked smaller and slighter. The form also claimed he was sickly, and he looked that too. But like the girl, he was better clothed than Kirstie. Peter decided he probably believed what she said, that she had begged only for the children and not for herself. He hoped for her sake that the Board would believe it: if they thought she had lived by begging, she would probably not get on to the poor roll.

They were strong on morality; the form also demanded to know if the applicant was a churchgoer. Kirstie looked, for the first time, conscious of her clothes; her actual reply was a keenly embarrassed glance at them and the comment: "I canna ging laek dis". Peter filled in the space, translating instinctively: *being unable to obtain decent clothes I have not for some time back attended the church. as I wished to do.*

When they were done, he gave her back the completed form to take to David Burns. She gazed, fascinated, at the mass of close writing.

"Will dey gie wis da room rent, d'ye tink?"

"I cudna say. They've let a good few on, but they're turning folk away in numbers too, I ken that. There's ower mony in need ... Still, ye've nae roof, they'll surely do something."

"I cud dae fine, if I just had da rent. I cud wirk an' feed me bairns, but a body canna spin ithout a room. "

"Have ye still got your furniture?"

"Aye, der's a neebir keepin' da tings fir me till I get a room again." Peter nodded. Landlords were getting warier, in these hard times; people who had fallen behind with the rent once too often were finding it difficult to get in anywhere else. But they always clung on to their bits of furniture, if they could. That way, they could tell themselves they were just between rooms; they still had a space to call their own, even if it didn't have four walls around it just then.

The boy leaning on the wall was taken with a fit of coughing; rasping and hollow. She called him over, and eased the little girl off her lap while she rubbed his back. Peter noticed that the boy's fingers were tracing letters on the form.

"D'ye go to the school?" he asked. The boy was shy of him and looked down, but Kirstie nodded proudly. "Aye, he's lernin' ta read. He's no' dere da day, becaas o' da bit o' a cough he has. If we had da room back, instead o' sleepin' ida rain, he'd be fine."

76

"Aye, like enough." On an impulse, he asked: "Does the neighbour let ye in sometimes?"

"Aye, we get a warm at her fire an' mak tea, whin I've got any."

"Go and get some, then; it'll maybe help him." He handed her some change; she smiled, and thanked him, with a remnant of country shyness that looked oddly like dignity.

He watched them go, wondering if she would get what she wanted out of the Board. She seemed so convinced that all would be well, if she just had a room to be sure of. It might be; despite her passive face and mild manner, the story on the form was that of a fighter. All the luck had gone against her so far, and she was still there; between rooms admittedly, but still keeping her family together. *I have had to beg for my children, or they could not have been alive.* He loved the way she had said that; neither passionately nor apologetically but quite simply, as a statement of fact, as a man might say he had done some heroic action because he had no other choice. He guessed it was in the same spirit that she had stolen for them.

He wondered why he had broken his own rule and given her money. He saw such people every day, and felt tempted to do the same, but mostly he managed not to, telling himself that once he started he would never stop. Maybe because she hadn't asked for it; maybe because he felt more admiration than pity for her. Or maybe because he suspected she wouldn't get it from the Board.

David Burns read the application form in the usual way, looking for the way out, the phrase that would identify someone else, rather than the Board, as liable. The form did not, in fact, require people to list their relatives and said relatives' trades out of idle curiosity; he had already been able to turn down one application that day on noting that the woman had a son-in-law doing well enough to help her. If she didn't get on with him, that was her problem. Kirstie's application dissatisfied him on two counts. She was not Lerwick-born, neither had her husband been; in all justice she and his child should be the responsibility of somebody up north, her home parish or her husband 's. And then there was this second child, who had a father living; he should be paying towards her keep. Burns read the little life story with distaste. It struck him as a record of ill-judgment and improvidence, the kind of steady slide which threatened to end in a permanent burden on the ratepayers. But not his ratepayers, if he could help it.

Unfortunately, though, nobody could deny that she and the children were currently in urgent need, which he had a legal duty to relieve. Reluctantly, he put them on interim relief at a shilling a month. Then he turned his mind to the more congenial duty of getting it back from somebody.

From the papers relating to her trial, he found that the Procurator Fiscal had been before him. Greig too had decided she must be the north's responsibility, and had even started a collection to get her repatriated there. But nothing seemed to have come of it — probably she had refused to go, thought Burns sourly; all these failed farmers thought they could live easier in Lerwick. With the second child's father, though, Greig seemed to have had more success: there was a note indicating that Caddel had made some sort of contribution to his daughter's living costs while her mother was imprisoned. This was encouraging; maybe the fellow just wanted reminding of his duties. Burns made a note to see him.

"No", said Caddel, flatly.

"Ye've no' denied ye're the father," protested Burns, "it's your responsibility."

"Da bairn's her midder's, no' mine. She doesna live wi' me; she'll no' wirk fir me whin she's aalder; why wid I pay fir her?

"Ye did when the mother was in Fort Charlotte."

"Aye, weel, she'd nabody else den." He forebore to mention that Archibald Greig was a far more forceful character than Burns and that it had been easier to give him what he wanted than to argue about it. "I'll pay, if I get her livin' wi' me."

"Well," Burns conceded, "there's some justice in that." Caddel shot him an incredulous, mocking glance. It was one of the oldest ploys in the book to offer maintenance only in return for custody; he hadn't actually expected the man to believe he meant it.

Burns was jotting down notes. "So, ye're willing to support the child, so long as the mother gives over care of her to you?"

"Oh, aye. Dat's right." Caddel could barely keep the contempt out of his voice; did the fool honestly think Kirstie would agree to that? For amusement, he added: "I cudna let da midder see her; she's no' a fit character, ye ken." Burns nodded seriously, and wrote it all down.

Charles Gilbert Duncan surveyed three cases, none of which he fancied working on especially, and wondered which he ought to start with. He was not sorry to see Andrew's face appear round the door.

"Aye, come and crack a while." He pushed the papers away from him and leaned back. "Are ye short of work, then?"

"No," Andrew said candidly, "just disinclined. I'd a case I cudna see my way forward with, and I took a strong dislike to the mere sight of the papers."

"What was it?"

"Och, just a poor old dame in dispute with her landlord. She'll be older yet, I doubt, the way the thing drags on."

Charles Gilbert raised an eyebrow. "Ye'll be working for no pay, I suppose."

"So do you, sometimes, and you've your sisters to look after. And a family some day, no doubt."

The younger man blushed slightly. "Aye, well, when my father died ... I'd no idea, ye ken, how much he did for the poor; there were folk on the Kirk poor-roll that listed him among their main sources of income."

"He was aye a kind man," said Andrew softly, "they'll be missing him, unless your Parochial Board's given them all an income for life yet."

Charles Gilbert laughed bitterly. "It'll be time to give the money out when we get our hands on it, I think. We've hardly considered any applicants yet; all we see at the meetings are letters from folk who don't want to pay the poor rate. He quoted contemptuously: *"Peter Morrison and others in Sound seek exemption on the ground of giving occasionally to the Poor in victuals.* Would ye credit that? When we met at the end of February, the treasurer had to tell us the funds from the Kirk were all used; he'd none from the rates yet, and the only way the people already on the poor roll would get paid on the first of March was if we passed the hat round! We had to levy a pound on each of the heritors and hope the ones who weren't there would agree to pay. I don't know if they have, yet."

Andrew whistled. "And these are the gentry that were so hot for leaving it all to charity! Ye'll no' be letting many on the roll, then?"

"David Burns is deciding that, mostly. It'll be well enough for the old sick folk, but I'd not care to be a man that canna find work, or someone from another parish." His eyes shifted to his papers; while they were talking he had seen the way to tackle one of his cases. His mind, unlike Andrew's, was seldom wholly away from his work.

In May, Burns told Kirstie he was stopping the temporary relief.

"Ye've no right claim on the Board; ye're a young woman able to work, and no' Lerwick-born either. If ye canna make enough with knitting and spinning, go out and do other work. Ye've a lad of eight; he could mind the other bairn."

"He's at da school!" She did not add that Jamie, with his remoteness and indifference, would make a poor baby-minder, even by eight-year-old standards. Burns shrugged.

"The truth is, your sort have no wish to work. I'd get you work myself, if I thought you'd take it."

"I'll tak any work, sae lang as I can bring me bairn or get her lookit efter."

But the inspector had already turned away, with a dismissive grunt; he hardly heard her answer. She glanced desperately around the room.

It was a general office; a few Sheriff Clerks were at work, but they avoided her eye.

Outside the office were a number of others who had failed to make it on to the roll. Some, like Kirstie, had young children to care for; some were men who could get no work. Margaret Anderson, the old widow, had been refused as being still in health and able to work. Most were bitter but despondent, feeling there was nothing to be done.

One man said he had heard you could take the Board to court and appeal against their decision. This was met with general ridicule. The Sheriff was not going to listen to poor folk, with the Board, people of his own kind, taking the other side. Any fool could see that. They dispersed, eventually, grumbling and ineffectual, talking about the Lord's will and drifting hopefully in the direction of the Street to see if they could beg anything.

Kirstie, however, had said nothing in answer to the man. With her experience of the law, she might have been expected to be afraid of it. In fact, she had never borne the court any ill-will about her sentence — after all, she had been guilty. What had impressed her above all was the fact that they had been willing to listen to her; she could never forget that they had asked her if she had anything to say.

She went back to Peter Williamson, to ask if he knew any lawyers.

Chapter 15
Lerwick: 1846-47

Andrew knew her as soon as she came in; she took longer to place him.

"Fort Charlotte", he prompted. "I spoke to you after ..." His voice trailed off awkwardly, but she nodded, without embarrassment. "I mind, ye, now."

A small, elegant bird, greyish-white with a dark head, lighted on the sill outside Andrew's window and began preening its elongated tail feathers. The dark-haired little girl on her mother's lap pointed and looked up, questioning.

"Tirrick[13]", Kirstie told her, "du kens it's simmer, whin dey come." The child slipped down and trotted over to look, Andrew's eyes following her. She was rather pretty, with delicate features, the dark hair and eyes startling against pale skin. He remembered the cotton frock, and the formal phrases of the indictment.

Kirstie asked timidly: "Can ye mak' dem let us on da poor-roll?"

"Maybe." He reached for the papers. "The Inspector'll say ye've no' looked for work and lived by begging."

She flushed. "I've aye wirked, whin dere wis a roof ower wis, an' wirk ta do. I can feed mesell an' da peerie eens; I just canna mak' enyoch ta pay da rent."

"And the begging?"

"No' till da lass wis born. Dey wir gude folk helped me; Sinclair Goudie an' Mr Angus' dochter. I didna' ask dem. But den da company failed; dere wisna muckle wark an' it wisna weel paid. An' ..." She paused, and gave the child a long, loving look. "Her fadir wudna ken her," she said bitterly, "an' a'body tocht waar o' me, fir we wirna mairrit ... An' if we've nae roof, I'll hae ta beg again. I canna wirk in da street, an' I canna let dem want."

"No," Andrew agreed. "Did ye say Sinclair helped? Would he speak for you, d'ye think?"

"Aye, but he went ta Scallowa, da same year."

"No, he's back now, just a few months ago. I'll have a word with him. Who else d'ye think would put in a word for you?"

13 "Tirrick" : Arctic Tern.

She thought. "Ye cud ask Jimmy Hunter. He wis da first we paid rent tae in Leerook, an' we paid aa we owed, afore we left da hoose.î
She smiled ruefully and Andrew laughed.

"I'll do my best, all right?"

She nodded. "I'd laek fine ta be in a room again," she said, and put her hands protectively over her stomach, "wi da bairn comin'."

"What?" He had not realised; it wasn't particularly noticeable yet. "Ye're having another? They'll want you to name the father, ye ken, in case he can pay."

"He died," she said softly, "he niver kent aboot da bairn. An' he wis just a young lad. John Irvine, dey caa'd him."

The name was familiar; Andrew thought back. John Thomas Irvine, if he remembered right, with a minor police record. He vaguely recalled a youth with a defiant grin, who seemed to loiter about doing nothing much for a living.

"He wis aaafil far frae his folk," she reminisced fondly, "an' he laekit ta come an' eat his denner wi wis, when we had da room."

No doubt, when he wasn't paying, thought Andrew. He felt a prickle of irritation with her, talking so indulgently of this wastrel who had taken advantage of her — and left her pregnant into the bargain; she'd certainly been unlucky there. But she looked content, rather than sorry.

"If it's a boy," she said, still caressing her stomach, "I'll ca' it Johnie, an' den he'll no' be forgotten."

Andrew closed his eyes briefly, as if in pain from the summer light, and thought about the dead, worthless, utterly enviable John Thomas Irvine.

"I'll get you all on the poor roll," he promised.

David Burns was furious about the court case. It was all wrong, this bringing the law into it. There was, there should be, a relationship of charity, be it from a board or an individual; what was given was a matter for the giver. When he heard that his decision — the Board's, since he was their servant — was to be challenged, he felt as if someone he had given, or refused to give, to had personally spat in his face. There was a ritual about these things, as prescribed as the steps of a dance: the giver gives, or chooses not to; the beggar waits on his decision; there is gratitude or resignation. He had noticed already the reaction of some of the paupers to his decisions — not acceptance but argument, not gratitude, often, but a taking for granted, as if he were giving them no more than their due. That was what came of institutionalising the money, instead of leaving it in individual hands to give.

He put together a hurried list, from memory, of the people who had given her clothes or food, her ex-landlords and anyone else he could think of who would tell the Sheriff what sort of person she was. He had so many other matters to consider that he gave little time to it; besides, he did not think it needed much time spent on it. He was certain none of his own kind would fail to see it the right way.

Some time later, Andrew Duncan, studying the papers for the hearing, ran his eye down Burns' list of witnesses and paused at one.

Charles Gilbert glanced up from his work at the familiar head round the door.

"I canna stop long to crack, Andrew."

"Och, this'll take no time at all. When ye were setting up the Parochial Board, was there no' someone stood against David Burns for Inspector?"

Charles Gilbert thought back. "Aye. Alex Nicol. He didna lose by all that many."

"I thought so." And the head retreated, leaving Charles Gilbert faintly puzzled.

Burns had known there would be no trouble with the landlords' evidence. They trooped up in a small, unpaid procession: Archibald Greig, William Sievwright and Jos Anderson, who had been her landlord when James died, and was still bitter that she hadn't left his loom to pay the debt. All eminently satisfactory, from Burns' point of view, though he was frankly baffled that it had been let go on so long. Greig's response when asked what steps he had taken to get his money back: *I did not press for it, as I conceived she was poor*, struck him as especially inappropriate for the Fiscal; what else was the law for? The other thing that puzzled him was the missing landlord, Sinclair Goudie, who he knew for a fact had lost money on her too, but was down as a witness for the other side. But then Goudie had always been a bit soft.

Burns allowed himself a little joke with Andrew Duncan after the landlords' testimony.

"You'll be waiting a long time for your fee, Andrew, if she treats you like her landlords."

Andrew grinned. "Aye, David, but ye see, if I win, you'll be paying me."

The trouble really started with the evidence of the people who had given her clothes. Beyond establishing that they had done so, Burns had never really questioned them himself. Certainly he was not ready for Andrew.

Ann Leslie Smith, watchmaker's wife: yes, she had given Kirstie clothes for the children.

"And tell me, Mrs Smith," Andrew enquired pleasantly, "did she ask you for the things or did you just give them out of kindness?"

"Och, she never asked. She had a sick bairn at the time, and they were awful ill off. I cud see that weel enough without being asked."

To Burns' annoyance, his next witness was asked the same question and gave the same answer. It was damaging, because part of his case was that she had lived by begging rather than find work. Still, there was no real cause for worry.

The next witness, Margaret Angus, did look as if she would do his case more good. She hesitated some time, then said reluctantly: "She would come around asking for clothes and food for the children; yes, I thought of her as a beggar."

"Was that the way of it when you started helping her?" Andrew asked quietly.

"No ... no, not at the first. She was left a widow, with a young child and another on the way. I made clothes for the baby, when he came, but she had not asked me to. She never begged then."

"When did she begin to beg?"

The girl paused a moment. "When the illegitimate child was born, I think."

"And then she begged for food and clothes for the child?"

"Yes."

"But when the earlier child was born she had not done so?"

"No."

"Because ..." he prompted.

"Because she did not need to," the girl said, very low.

Burns' last witness was Alex Nicol. Though the name meant nothing to Kirstie, his face looked vaguely familiar. But she could not place him, until the Sheriff asked if it were true, as the Inspector alleged, that she had refused work.

"I heard the Inspector offer to give work to the applicant, and she said she would come."

She knew him then; he had been one of the Sheriff Clerks in the office, when Burns refused to help her.

Burns was furious. His recollection might not be exact, but he was certain she had made some sort of feeble excuse, probably about the children. Anyway, Alex should understand what side he was meant to be on. He cursed himself for not having checked his witnesses; he had never imagined the hearing would be more than a formality. He could hear Sinclair Goudie now, testifying that she had worked for a living as long as he was her landlord: *She was occupied spinning, knitting and other such employment as she could get ... she suffered much distress and received charity from me without asking for it.*

Burns glanced at the paper in front of him, detailing the money she had already been given by the town: three shillings out of the kirk collection when James died, three and six to bury Magnus; how long had it taken to get that back from Northmavine, and as for the fourteen shillings it had cost to board the children while she was in jail, they'd never see the colour of that again .... He knew his case had not gone as well as it should. But like the rejected applicants outside his office, he still thought the court would side with its own kind. When Sheriff Bell found in favour of the applicant, Burns could not, at first, take it in.

The applicant. It wasn't just the ratepayers' money, though here were three more on the poor roll — and the woman, he noted with disgust, about to have another. It was the principles at issue. The Board had been told it had a duty to incomers from another parish; to an able-bodied adult who had problems finding work, and to a child whose father wouldn't support it — Caddel had lately done ten days in prison, rather than pay up. Had the court, Burns wondered, any idea what a precedent it was setting? If the Board were to work to these criteria, there might soon be more on the roll than paying the rates. No, they'd have to appeal. If nothing else, he thought with grim satisfaction, it would delay the payment of Andrew Duncan's bill.

It was a few days later, at a party in someone's house, that Andrew met Margaret Angus again.

"I thought ill of myself," she said with her customary directness, "about that woman. You were right; she'd not have begged, and maybe not stolen either, if she could have got help without."

"Och, I never meant you should feel at fault. I ken fine how much you did for her."

"Aye ... but it's true I could never like her as well after she took up with that man. I couldn't but feel it was so unfitting a widow, somehow."

"Well," Andrew said gently, "faithful widows are fine and romantic, but they maybe get awful lonely."

"She said something like that; they all say it, women like her, but surely the finer feelings ... If *you* were widowed, now, you'd not think anyone could replace *your* wife; you'd be content to remember her."

She spoke with all the certainty of the emotionally inexperienced, and it occurred to Andrew that romantic novels had a lot to answer for. Briefly his mind rested on the picture she had sketched; Catherine gone and him alone in a wide bed, warming himself with memories ... He nearly told her: not on a winter night, but thought better of it. She was just a young woman, hardly more than a girl; she had a right to be innocent and idealistic. Curiously enough, she reminded him a little of Kirstie and her romantic indulgence of shiftless Irvine, the boy far from his folks who'd needed feeding.

About the end of December, Charles Gilbert's head appeared round Andrew's office door.

"You should be seeing the colour of your money from the Board soon; they've seen sense and dropped the appeal. I've been telling them for months they'd no case."

"She and the bairns'll be safe on the poor roll, then. She must have had the baby by now. D'ye know if it was a boy?"

Charles Gilbert laughed. "I've no notion. Why, were ye hoping she'd call it Andrew?"

Chapter 16
Lerwick: 1847-9

There was a soup kitchen in Lerwick now. The Shetland potato crop failed, struck by the same blight that had hit Ireland the year before. From all over the countryside, crofters who normally relied on a loft full of tatties to see them through the winter drifted to the town, either hoping things would be better there or knowing that at least they could be no worse. The soup had to be bought with tickets; they cost little, but many still had not the price, and there was fierce competition for the free tickets that were handed out to the destitute.

The ladies ran the kitchen, and gave out the tickets; they had organised themselves into a committee. Lerwick was full of committees these days. Andrew Duncan, who had once reckoned himself such a non-committee man, had actually been instrumental in setting one up. It was trying to finance temporary work , like road-building, by raising subscriptions and any other means it could think of, such as applying to funds elsewhere in Britain, or persuading private businesses to help — Andrew's latest dream was a joint-stock company to provide new industries.

They had tried asking the Treasury for finance, and got nowhere. But there was a new board in Edinburgh now, for relieving destitution in the Highlands and Islands, which they had more hopes of. At least, it had sent an inspector, an ex-navy man called Craigie. Andrew hadn't met him yet; as soon as he arrived he had set off to tour the whole island group. A thorough man, by all accounts. Andrew hoped he was also a susceptible one. The committee had made up a list of men seeking work; there were entries on it he couldn't get out of his head. *Jethro Sandison, 16, living by the docks, large family to support and father absent.* Some were on the poor roll; most desperately wanted not to be. He remembered his father's indignant defence of them to the Royal Commission: "They would work willingly, if there was work to be had."

Andrew's face softened; his father had died that year, and he knew that was part of the reason for his involvement with the committee, just as Charles Gilbert had become active on the Parochial Board partly in honour of his own father's abundant charity. He still liked to put his head round Charles Gilbert's door, when he had the time to spare from committees and casework. The saga of the old woman in dispute with her landlord was still dragging on; they chatted about that sometimes, or swapped stories from their committees.

"Ye'll like this one," Charles Gilbert leaned back in his chair. "The Remarks of David Burns, no less, who has been ruminating on the condition of the paupers and is pleased to let the Board have his views on the same. Listen to this one, Andrew." He read with relish, in a fair imitation of Burns' slightly sniffy, precise tones: *Parties who are allowed 1/4d and 2/8d monthly cannot be said to be depending on that source for aliment. Such an allowance can only be supposed to pay their share of a rent, or procure them clothing, and the less provident among them, I have no doubt, deem it so trifling that they apply it at once in purchase of some luxury.*

He had given "luxury" a perfect intonation of Calvinistic distaste, and Andrew laughed delightedly. "What's he want you to do about it?"

"Oh, pay them quarterly. He wants all the allowances revised downwards as it is; apparently food's costing less this year. But according to him it's all their own fault anyway; listen: *Many of the paupers are living in miserable hovels, which affects their health much, from a vitiated inclination to live in dirt and among dirty wretches.*

"God almighty! And his old sinner of a father owns the worst of them!" Andrew picked up a pencil from the desk and snapped it without thinking. "Sorry, Charles. He's no' the right man for Inspector, that's sure. You'd do it better."

Charles Gilbert made a face. "I've no fancy for it. And there's no' enough the Inspector can do, nor the Board even, for that matter. I'd sooner be somewhere I can make a real difference to the town." He paused, and said diffidently: "I was thinking of maybe standing for the Council soon."

"Aye, of course ye should. After all, Gilbert was years on the council, and we're both in our fathers' place now, in a manner of speaking. As much as I could ever be, anyway."

Charles Gilbert put a hand on his arm. "I ken ye miss him. I mind when it was mine."

"Aye. I'll tell you one thing, though: I'd miss him less if I'd bairns of my own. It wasna meant to be, for me and Catherine, but with you it looks like being your own choice. No, hear me, Charles; ye're gone thirty and there's no' just work in life."

"Och, I'll get around to marrying. When I've got my sisters settled, maybe, and less work on."

"Maybe." Andrew's face was troubled. "I just don't like to think of you lonely, that's all. Folk get old quicker than they think for. God, I'll be fifty soon enough."

"Aye, and still at law with the old dame's landlord."

Andrew grinned, and threw the bits of pencil at him.

David Burns took sick and died in the spring of 1848; probably, Samuel Henry opined, of something he caught from a pauper. The thought did not deter Henry, a few months later, from offering himself as Inspector. Charles Gilbert was no longer so surprised anyone would want the job. There was undoubtedly a feeling of power attached to it, if you enjoyed having power over folk who were relatively so helpless. It wasn't the sort of power he wanted, but some would. Henry was an arrogant man, though, and in the end the Inspector was only the Board's servant; Charles couldn't see him sticking it for too long.

If they had had to lose his services as Clerk, the Board might have looked askance at the change; it was worth something to have the papers always in good order, and the minutes in his clear, exquisite hand. But he offered to do both jobs. That, at least, did impress Charles Gilbert, with his own inexhaustible appetite for work; he even agreed there might be some sense in raising the salary to £25. As Henry said, it was really not that much considering the responsibilities of the post.

It was summer: the days were long and light, the nights more blue than black. The docks were busy with shipping, and many of the men had found work on the new roads that Captain Craigie was having built. Apart from money, the Government had provided soldier engineers; when they blasted their way through rock, the sound sometimes carried all the way to town. Like Yule at the wrong time of year, as someone remarked in the well queue.

That was the drawback of summer; there was usually a queue for the well, but these days it was a fairly good-humoured one. The extra work got the men out of the house and improved their mood, and that rubbed off on the women. And the more folk in work, the better for the merchants, and for the price of knitting and spinning. As she waited her turn, Kirstie closed her eyes, lifted her face to the sun and smiled. Her expression was starting to relax, to lose the tension of recent years; she was beginning to feel safe.

Henry had not been long in office before he had a purge of the poor-roll, and able-bodied mothers with young children were a group for whom he had no sympathy whatever. He had struck numbers of them off, in May, but Kirstie knew what to do now. She simply went back to the Sheriff Court, who made an order instructing the Board to relieve her.

She was on a shilling a week, plus 1s 4d a month from the bitterly resentful Caddel (once the Board knew the problem of Kirstie was not going to go away, they had pursued him for his share with much more vigour). In effect, it meant she could pay the rent. Now there was a better market for handwork, she could feed the children by it; even keep Jamie and peerie Kirstie at the school with the odd bit of help from folk who gave her decent clothes for them. But she would never make enough to pay the rent, not without the Board's help. Still, things were looking none so bad. Jamie was eleven now, maybe soon he could get work and help her. Peerie Kirstie, seven now, had started at the school too; her mother, glancing guiltily down at her, knew her bit of a cough was not really bad enough for her to have stayed off today. She liked the child's company, that was the fact of it, and peerie Kirstie was so good with the little one ....

She had let him off the leash now, though; while his mother daydreamed he had found a puddle, and toddled up to her all over mud. She exclaimed, horrified, and he glanced at her under his eyelashes and grinned. The other women waiting laughed, and so did she. Johnie, at three, had a smile as endearing as his late father's had been. Anyway she felt disinclined to be cross with anyone, what with the rent safe and the sun still warm on her eyelids. Light always made her happy.

Samuel Henry was in less of a good mood. Kirstie's success in the Sheriff Court was only one of a string of reverses in what was turning out to be a bad year. The Board, not wanting to be on the wrong end of any more legal actions, were getting less inclined to back his judgement; it seemed, lately, that he only had to report a refusal of relief to someone undeserving for them to take fright and countermand him. There was a man a few months back, wanting temporary relief because he was off work with a broken arm; a clear case, one would have said, of a man who shouldn't be encouraged to become dependent. Henry had thought it would suffice simply to report his refusal, as a formality, to the Board. But no; he'd been told to give the fellow 1s 4d a week and let him pay it off once he was working again. If he ever did. Sometimes he thought it would be simpler not to report things to them at all.

Of course they were terrified of the Board of Supervision in Edinburgh. His face darkened at the mere thought of that body; he had already had one run-in with them. There was a woman, one of the sort that wander from place to place and do no good in any of them; she had tried her luck in Scotland but had come back that year. To Lerwick, of course, though she came from the south of the island somewhere. He had turned down her request for help, not thinking her any of his responsibility; nor did he think any differently about it now she was dead. The letter from Edinburgh hadn't worried him, because he still thought he was right; he merely felt the bitterest resentment at its tone. *I am to remind you of your imperative duty to provide lodging, food, medical and all other needful relief to a poor person applying to you for relief in the parish, who is a fit object of relief.* This in a letter from one gentleman to another.

He pushed the letter impatiently from him, and took up something which pleased him better: David Burns' paper, that he'd submitted for the Board's consideration before he died. Poor David; no doubt he'd felt just as frustrated with a Board that wouldn't back him, and busybodies in Edinburgh deciding who was a fit object of relief. But he had been a weak man, who eventually settled for being the Board's servant and no more. Henry thought the job was capable of better.

His eye skimmed the paper: *the number of people who have been intimating that they intend applying for relief is fearful to contemplate; in fact every feeling of pride in being above soliciting parochial aid seems to be fast breaking up among the lower classes, most of them speaking of it not now as charity but as a right to which they are legally entitled.*

Aye, well, that came of bringing the law into it. The Sheriff Court order about Kirstie was one setback among many, but it was one which particularly annoyed him. Back in Burns' time, she had been the first to take the Board to court and win; others had done it since who might never have tried it without her example. Like Burns, he found himself offended by the more notion of someone in her position doing that; seeking to establish as a right what he still saw as a favour, and one which, left to himself, he would never have given her. It annoyed him even more that she had now done it to him.

Thinking about her, which he didn't do more than he could help, he was puzzled. She looked as timid, passive and whey-faced as all the other paupers he encountered, yet somewhere there was this well-spring of defiance which struck him as altogether improper and vaguely disorderly. He had passed her in the Street that morning, with her children, and she had been looking at them with an expression which could only be described as pride. Henry knew pride when he saw it; none better, and he knew that when he contemplated his handsome, fashionable daughters, the look in his eyes was exactly the one in Kirstie's. And two of hers without fathers, and she not able to care for them without the ratepayers' money ....

She had smiled calmly at him, when she caught his eyes fixed on her. He took it for insolence, but it had not in fact been so intended. Kirstie was happy because it was a sunny day, and proud, because she and her children hadn't gone to the wall yet, which considering everything struck her as something of an achievement. And calm, because it looked as if things would be all right. She knew Henry disliked her; so had Burns if it came to that, but because the law was there, it didn't really matter. So she smiled at him, generously, like a good winner.

PART FIVE

CHURCH LANE

Chapter 17
Lerwick: 1851

The renaming committee of '45 had christened it Church Lane, but for many it was still South Kirk Closs. The young clerk, writing up his notes for the 1851 census, recalled it with a grimace. It was strange how the lanes, which shared so many problems, were yet unlike. One would be sober, another noisy; in one, nearly every family would have some work and money coming in, while in the next one along, half the population was on the parish.

Church Lane was one of the oldest; it took its name from the outgrown kirk at its top end, which had been turned into the Subscription Rooms. It was one of the longest-inhabited streets in town, which was presumably why, unlike most of the lanes, it had actually acquired some paving. It had no other obvious advantage. The houses were showing their age; the largest ones, let out to several families, looking ill-cared-for. Every room in every house was full, and the sheer numbers made it unusually dirty, even for a Lerwick lane; there were middens and refuse tips all over the cracked, uneven stones. Some of the more respectable tenants towards the Commercial Street end were still making a valiant effort to keep up appearances, but it was not the sort of place which gave you much incentive for that. It had a discouraged, and discouraging, air; it was an address you gravitated slowly down to as times grew worse; a badge of failure.

The clerk began to get his notes in order, trying to relate the names on the page to the people he had seen and questioned. Andrew Hay, retired India merchant, with his wife and an impossibly ancient mother-in-law. Martha Randall, pauper and stocking-knitter. It was common for a woman to be listed as head of household; there were so many widows, like Charlotte Thomson, or wives like Isabella Robertson, waiting for absent sailors.

He paused at an unusually long entry. He recallled the house: taller than most, on a slight curve; one of William Hay's buildings, let out to an assortment of tenants. The usual professions: Margaret Garrick, sailor's wife, with three daughters at the stocking-knitting; Laura Williamson, widow, making a living at wool spinning; not much of one, he guessed, recalling the bare room. William Simpson the shoemaker, painfully respectable in the midst of squalor, he and his oldest son both trying to make a living out of what business there was and feed the younger children. Barbara Matthewson and three children; another widow? No: he remembered now; the husband was a convict in Van Diemen's Land. None of the children in school, he noticed. And another widow, Christina Jamieson, with three children, the two eldest down as "scholars", which probably meant they were going to the parochial school at the top of Mounthooly Street, though how regularly was another matter. Often, attendance depended on whether children were needed at home to look after younger ones, or had got casual work for the day, or had no clothes fit to go in.

He totted up all the widows and stocking-knitters, scholars and paupers, lodgers fitting somehow into the corner of a room already occupied by a family of six. There were twenty-three in that house — William Hay would make another fortune at this rate, assuming he could get his rents paid. Of course he lived outside town himself, though he'd been counted for the census at his office in Commercial Street.

The young man's finger traced down the line of the Street on his map, remembering the households he had checked. No. 3; Andrew Duncan's office; he and Catherine were still alone in the big house that echoed with the lack of children. Just over the road at no. 6 was his cousin Charles Gilbert, with two of his sisters to keep house for him. Further along still was the young Procurator Fiscal, Archibald Greig, with three infant sons. The clerk traced up respectable Hill Lane: Dr Cowie with his wife, Greig's sister, and their four sons; Sinclair Goudie, grocer and spirit dealer, with a rackety houseful of children, servants, lodgers and visitors; nobody seemed sure exactly how many were under the roof, but Sinclair had been generous with the spirits while they were finding out.

He smiled in memory, but then put the map aside; he knew he was only delaying writing up the rest of Church Lane. The truth was, it depressed him even to think about the place.

Kirstie, knitting at her window, might have been surprised that he thought so poorly of it. She had lived in worse places, notably the street, and she no longer cared much what kind of a room she lived in, providied she was sure of still being there after next rent day. Thanks to the law, it seemed she no longer had to worry about that. Kirstie and the Board existed in an uneasy truce; they paid the rent while she fed and clothed the children on what she could earn. She knew well enough that Samuel Henry resented every penny the Board gave her; he left her in no doubt of it every time he saw her, which was quite often, as his office was at the top of the lane. But she knew too that the Board had had enough of going to law, and had overruled him on a couple of occasions when he had cut off the allowance. She would never get ahead of the game, as she and James had once hoped; she accepted that now. But she felt safe, and would settle for that.

Her major worry at that time, in fact, was Jamie. He was thirteen, still at the school (thanks partly to Margaret Angus); he could read and write better than his mother ever would. But though he looked more like his father every day, she could see nothing of James in him. There was no energy, no adventure, no belief in himself or anyone else. Trying to see what she wished, she reasoned that it was partly his health; he'd never been the same since the smallpox. Which was true, but neither had she, and it hadn't prevented her from working and surviving for ten years, because she had to.

She hardly knew what Jamie felt, about anything. He watched things happen, people come and go, without comment or appparent interest. He rarely quarrelled with his brother and sister, but rarely showed affection either. His mother was an exception, she knew he did care for her, but she sometimes wondered if he wished he didn't. What worried her most was the way he felt about his own life. He seemed to have no hope that things could ever be any better, and certainly no belief that he himself could ever change them.

She did wonder sometimes if it had to do with how he had grown up. But she recalled Laurie Laurenson at thirteen; sharp, hard-bitten, cynical indeed, like Jamie, but far from having given up. And there was Johnston, her neighbour Baubie's eldest lad; he ran errands and helped with the bills when he could ... Well, he was fifteen; maybe when Jamie was older he would see things differently.

For the first time in years, she thought of Robert and his patient, hopeless eyes.

The light was going; she rose and kindled the kollie lamp, with its smell of fish-liver-oil that always hung about the room. There was a pain in her side when she moved, where her breathing caught her, and she felt tired. Johnie and peerie Kirstie, playing on the floor, got bored with their game and started a quarrel. She shushed them.

"Whit else can we play?"

She thought a moment, back to the games she had played with Mary in the croft. "Row da boats?" They looked uncomprehending, and she realised it was one she hadn't taught them. She couldn't recall who had taught it to her — Hercules maybe, or Anne, or some old quarter-wife sitting in the corner, or even Robert in one of his rare idle moments. There was nearly always someone on a croft who had time for that sort of thing, even if the mother was busy.

Sometimes when she sang songs or told them riddles, she would see them baffled by some object, or bird-name, or pattern of behaviour, which had been part of her childhood, but had no place in the town.

Something like a corn hook, or a candle in a cow's skull. Usually, then, she felt guilty and tried to do something about it. She even retold Hercules' stories.

" ...An' he telt me ance, dere wir places whaur da trees wir as big as a hoose."

"Aye", said Jamie, with a complete lack of wonder, "dey telt wis dat ida school".

"Is du shure?"

"Aye. I'm seen picters."

She was amazed, not only that it was true, for she had long been convinced it was one of Hercules' fancies, but by the casualness with which the children accepted it. It was of a piece with the writing, which even peerie Kirstie was learning now; the incomprehensible syllables held no mystery for them. She was abashed, sometimes, to think how much more they knew than her.

Next day she mentioned it ruefully to Margaret Cheyne, her neighbour from three doors up. Margaret nodded. Though, like Kirstie, she was about thirty-eight, she had married late; her Janet was some years off the school yet.

"I want her to go, dat's shure," she conceded, "but it'll be strange when she can write an' I canna."

They were leaning against the house-front, chatting, while peerie Kirstie played gently with Janet; she liked small children. Baubie Matthewson, on her way to the Baker's Well, caught the tail-end of Margaret's remark.

"A' da lernin's no' in books." Baubie couldn't write either, or read much, but she refused to be ashamed of it — or of being on the poor-roll, or of her man in Van Diemen's Land. She was abrasive and hard-bitten, a kind of grown-up Laurie, but Kirstie liked her for being a fighter. Her journey to Lerwick had been longer even than Kirstie's; she came from Unst, the windy northernmost isle in the group. Sometimes she would mock Kirstie's complaints about the cold; no-one from Lerwick, she claimed, had any notion of what real cold was.

It hadn't occurred to Kirstie to say she wasn't from Lerwick either. She had only been there about eleven years; she had spent more than twice that time in the country. But Lerwick was where James and Magnus had died, where she had kept her children together and brought them up, and worked out how to get by on her own. Even the Parochial Board had stopped suggesting she go back north; she herself knew she could live nowhere else but here.

A red-capped man turned into the lane from the Street, walking with the easy swing of a sailor. Baubie, who was forty-five if she was a day, eyed him appreciatively and made a mildly lewd remark; he grinned and replied in kind, but it was Kirstie he wanted. He showed her some trifles, carved from whalebone or walrus tusk.

"D'ye want ta sell dem?" "Aye, shure." "Come eftir da money da nicht."

She could hardly remember, now, how she had once feared the foreign sailors. They were decent lads enough, mostly, but they did tend to run out of cash while they were in port. That was when they would sell their carvings, or any other goods that would get them the price of drink, or whatever else they wanted. Half of them had no idea what the going rate was, and would gladly pay a bit in commission to a local who would act as agent, get them a fair price and pay over the money honestly. It was hardly a steady job, but in the season it came in handy sometimes.

She left peerie Kirstie minding Johnie and went down the Street to sell the trinkets and a bit of spinning; not as much as it should have been. She found, nowadays, that she could not sit down to it for long without getting pains in her back.

It was lamplight when the sailor came for his money. Kirstie reached up to the shelf where she had put it by for him, while he exchanged a few words with Jamie in what she took to be Dutch or German. Jamie had a little of both; people brought up in Lerwick often did.

She saw him out at the door, and as his boots clattered off down the stairs, she noticed William Simpson, her neighbour from across the passage, looking disapprovingly from his own doorway. He was a kind man, was William, but with a narrow notion of respectability, and she knew he would only be able to think of one reason for a woman to be visited by sailors. Maybe she could have explained, but she hardly liked to, and he might not have believed her.

Besides, he would not always have been wrong. Once or twice, when Henry was having another try at cutting off the allowance and she needed money in a hurry, she had got it that way. It was not something she could ever fancy as a trade, but if the children were in need there was no choice; there was never a choice. *I have had to beg for my children, or they could not have been alive.* Or you stole clothes from washing-lines, or pestered the Parochial Board, or simply worked when you felt like resting; what was a sailor more or less?

Chapter 18
Lerwick: 1851-2

In his office in the Subscription Rooms, Samuel Henry reluctantly turned his mind from a Wick newspaper's rapturous account of the Great Exhibition and went back to writing up the Parochial Board minutes. Applicants for relief: Barbara Bain, sixty-three and ill: *the Board considering that this woman is not very aged and may recover her usual strength do not deem it expedient at present to place her on the Roll as a permanent pauper.* Mary Tait's coffin, allowed at eight-and-six, she having made no demands upon the Board though a helpless person for some time. Grizel Cogle: to be removed from the Roll; her allowance had been reduced and she'd written the Board a rude letter about it.

More successful appeals to the Sheriff Court: he hated recording in the minutes that the Board had received yet another order to relieve someone they had turned down. It was happening far more frequently, these days.

The Lindsay case: that was the letter from the Gorbals Parochial Board, asking for help to fight an appeal case in the House of Lords "on the question of right to parochial relief by all able-bodied persons out of employment", if you could credit that such a thing had ever got so far. They had sent five pounds ten.

And Christina Inkster ... He nearly went back to the newspaper; he had a physical aversion to recording his defeats, especially those that involved her. *The Inspector reported that he had discontinued the weekly allowance to Christina Inkster, as also that he had not paid any rent for her since Candlemas last, until he should receive direction from the Board. The Meeting considering that it will still be necessary to continue some aid to the said Christina Inkster in respect of her youngest son authorised the Inspector to pay the house rent since Candlemas last and continue the allowance to her at the rate of 9s per quarter to meet her rent till farther orders.*

He was tempted to scribble it illegibly, but he had too much pride in his handwriting for that. There were cases which he was beginning to despair of making the Board see as he did. His eye fell again on the Exhibition report. The great glass palace, full of wonder and enterprise, visited by millions, sending its declaration of cultural and commercial supremacy all over the world. He kindled at the thought of the age he lived in; its opportunity, its achievement. It was an age to succeed in, if you were at all worth while; there had to be something amiss, he felt, with anyone who couldn't make their way in a world like this.

Kirstie and Baubie, their shopping done, wandered home along the Street and indulged themselves looking at all the things they couldn't afford. The bolts of bright cloth, the gold watches, tortoiseshell combs, scented oils and soaps, ornately framed looking-glasses in which they caught sight of their own middle-aged, lined faces and laughed at the comically wide-eyed expression in them. Six-year-old Johnie was in front, constantly running back to tell them of the latest marvel he'd seen; Kirstie recalled, with something of a pang, when Jamie had been like that.

Window-shopping did not make her feel bitter or deprived. The glittering goods behind the glass were a display, something to brighten up the street; she did not regard them in the light of things you might actually buy or exchange for knitting. She would have been sorry not to see them, for they were pleasant to the eye and you could feast your imagination on them. Deprived was what she felt when she hadn't enough to buy tatties.

Baubie nudged her. "Dere's Keetie, da waar o' drink again."

A young woman, about twenty-five, was coming down the Street, swaying slightly and putting out a hand to the wall now and then. Some way behind her, a two-year-old stumbled along, trying to keep up. Kirstie looked at him with pity. The young woman intercepted the glance and flared up.

"He's no' wantin' pity frae da laeks o' dee! At least we're no' on da parish."

"No' as lang as da hoorin 'll pay fir da drink," murmured Baubie. The woman made a brief face in her direction, but all her attention was on Kirstie, who, still looking at the boy, said "Du shudna drink, whin du's da bairn ta mind."

The woman let fly a rain of curses, with a vehemence the drink could not altogether account for. Baubie laughed and gave her some back, but it was Kirstie she was still shouting at, as they walked away from her.

Kirstie was a peaceable neighbour; she could get on with almost anyone. Apart from Jerome Caddel, she would have been hard put to it to think of someone in town she disliked; nor did many apart from Henry actually dislike her. Katie Laing was an exception. Despite Baubie's crack about the whoring, neither she nor Kirstie would really have been judgemental about that — you could never tell what you yourself might be forced to do, to feed yourself or your children. Not, as Baubie caustically remarked, that Katie's boy would ever see much of her profits. It was well known that when the census man came round, last year, the child had been six months old, and she still hadn't got around to giving him a name.

Her indifference to her child, and her drinking, would always have provoked Kirstie, but she had seen bad mothers before; nor were all her friends averse to a drink; if she was being honest she might have admitted there was something else about Katie. The girl was a prostitute by trade; Kirstie still saw herself as a housewife, or wanted to. Maybe, too, it worked the other way. As Katie had claimed, she wasn't on the parish, but she and her old, invalid father were not far from it. Her sister had escaped to Edinburgh and left it all behind. Kirstie, stuck on parish relief for so long with no way out, must have looked like the pattern of her future. Her mother's name had been Christina, as it happened.

Kirstie and Baubie strolled home companionably, talking about their children and the difficulty of getting money out of the Board. "But dey'll gie me whit I'm askin' noo," Baubie said confidently.

"Whit's dat?"

"Da fare ta Glesca[14], so we can ging ta Van Diemen's Land."

"Du's jokin'!"

"I'm no' jokin'. Me man's free sune, an' dere's some board in Glesca dat helps folk laek wis get oot dere. Dey'll gie wis da money fir dat, shure enyoch; dey'll aye pay ta get rid o' wis."

"It's an aafil lang wye," said Kirstie timidly.

Baubie shrugged. "So was Unst. Dere's nathin' fir wis here."

Kirstie thought about it. Lots of people emigrated, she knew, though few went as far as that. But some went to America, and many down south to Scotland, where there was supposed to be more work and better pay. It was only what she and James had done, in a way. Of course Baubie had to go where her man was, just as she had had to follow James. (When she first applied for parochial relief, one of the questions on the form had been: why did you come to town? She had furrowed her brow, puzzled, and replied: "I cam' wi' me man," which Peter Williamson duly translated as: "My husband thought proper to remove to Lerwick and I accompanied him.")

Maybe she was less adventurous now, but she knew she could not face starting again anywhere else, even if it were better. She would miss Baubie for a neighbour. So many people, since she came to town; so many faces that were part of your life for a while and then moved on. She had a sudden brief vision of them all: Ann, Laurie, David Burns with his thin smile and Sinclair Goudie with his generous one; James and Magnus; Jimmy Hunter who still gave her a friendly word now and then and Jerome Caddel whom she passed on the street in a bitter, speaking silence. John Irvine, whose chirpy, little-boy grin was on the

14 "Glesca" : Glasgow.

102

face of her child .... As James' features, so long rubbed out, had been made again in Jamie; as her own were mirrored in the daughter of the man who had wanted no likeness, and had none.

Charles Gilbert slit open a letter, glanced over its contents and sighed. It was the outcome, at long last, of Andrew's long-running lawsuit on behalf of the old woman in dispute with her landlord. It had gone in favour of her in the end, Charles Gilbert noted; a pity Andrew would never know. They had joked, sometimes, that the old lady might not live to see the end of it, but things had turned out otherwise.

Charles Gilbert was Procurator Fiscal now. It was a new departure; the first job he had tackled which neither his father nor his uncles had done before. But Archibald Greig, who seemed to do everything at too young an age, had died at thirty-two, leaving three infant sons. Charles Gilbert shivered slightly. The extra work came welcome to him. Whenever he lost concentration for a while, he found himself glancing at the door, waiting for Andrew's familiar head to appear round it. There was a corner of his desk which he still tended to keep clear of papers, as if someone might want to perch on it. At home, he had only just got around to sitting in his father's armchair, and was surprised to find he fitted it.

Like Kirstie, he sometimes found his mind running on a procession of people: Gilbert, Charles Ogilvy, the Sheriff, Andrew the cousin who'd been old enough to be yet another father .... When he was young, the landscape of his life had been full of such figures; by and by they had become fewer and more shadowy, until now he realised with a slight start that he himself was next in the line, the one his younger relatives wanted to emulate.

He was thirty-six, and still unmarried. He had not forgotten Andrew's warnings about loneliness, and the way the aching want of children could catch up with you. He thought of it sometimes when he saw Archibald's old father out walking with his little grandsons. But his own reaction to a void in his life had always been to pour work into it, and the truth was that the work fascinated him for its own sake too.

What with his work on the Town Council and the Fiscal's job, he saw little of the Parochial Board now, except when he drew their attention to someone who needed relief. But though individuals still mattered to him (he did as much legal work free of charge as Andrew had), he had a wider idea, now, of what he wanted for the town. He wanted gas lighting and a better police force, to discourage crime; clean water and a sewerage sytsem, to kill off the fever; paving, improvements ... He was as partisan about the town as his father and uncles had been, and more determined to make his ideas happen. He could not imagine the person complex and fascinating enough to absorb him the way this town, its problems and its future did.

Besides, his sisters were still content to keep house for him, and if you had a family to think of, you could get so much less done.

Sometimes he would go up the Hillhead, or to Fort Charlotte, just to look down at the town. He would scan the close, dark, foetid lanes, imagining air and light into them; pave over in his mind the muddy streets, think grass and flowers into the abandoned kirkyard where the refuse of Church Lane was thrown. From the Fort he could see Freefield, slowly building up business again, and his thoughts would go to Charles Ogilvy, who could not survive the breaking of dreams. He had told some of them to his nephew, here, looking out over the sea-roads crowded with shipping, to the northern sky that was never bland or cloudless for long, but full of change and activity.

Ogilvy had once looked out, like this, and felt the town and all its fortunes and all its people rush in on him, as if they were his intimate concern. Andrew too. It had happened suddenly to them, like falling in love, and they had never been quite the same again. Ogilvy had died because he felt he could do nothing for the object of his affections, and Andrew had maybe shortened his life trying.

But it had happened differently to Charles Gilbert; his feeling for the place had insinuated itself into his being like sunlight into skin, or some climbing plant that eases itself uninvited into the cracks of a wall, until its tendrils are what holds the stone together. He did not so much feel that he loved it, as know that it was part of him, or his life part of it; it was less a lover than an old friend whose very faults meant more to him than the virtues of strangers.

Chapter 19
Lerwick: 1853

Kirstie had slipped out before the children woke, to avoid the well queue. Standing about waiting did her back no good, and the cold always seemed to get to her lungs. It was better to go in the half-light, when not many were about. She met only a few sleepy maids, who had to rise early so that all would be in order by the time their employers came down.

It was so early that the scavengers were still out in the Street with their brooms, spades and barrows. The Police Commission paid them to do what they could to keep it clean. They tended to be oldish men who weren't fit for heavier work, or could get none better — it took a strong stomach, if nothing else. She flattened herself against a shop wall, to let one go by.

As he passed, eyes fixed on the ground, she gave him a second look — she surely knew him from somewhere. She tried to picture him in some building she'd lived in, or working down at the docks, or even in Fort Charlotte prison, but he fitted nowhere. He made his slow way off down the Street, stooping at every moment to sweep rubbish aside or shovel dung into the barrow — there was a market for that; the Commission sold it — and she stared after him, still baffled.

Then a woman went by with a basket of peats, and the earthy smell, stronger for a moment than those of the Street, carried her memory back to the place where he fitted: why, he didn't belong in Lerwick at all; he was one of the Andersons from Olnafirth, where she and James had farmed when they were first married. He looked older though — but of course he would; that was fifteen years ago, she realised with a small shock. She called out to him: "Tammas!" and he turned, jumpily, as if he dreaded to be recognised. Yet there was relief in his eyes too, at seeing a known face; she could tell he remembered her.

"Whit's du in Lerook for, Tammas?"

"We wir pitten oot." His voice had a slow burr to it which took her back years; it was so like James, who had never been in Lerwick long enough to acquire the quicker, harsher accent of the town. She put a hand on his arm in sympathy.

"Cud du no' pay da rent?"

He shook his head. The day was brightening; a shaft of early sun struck between two tall buildings and turned the twigs of his broom golden, as if they had caught light. He stared at the flash of colour on the grey pavement, like a man gazing into a fire to get warm.

"Wis du no' heard, ida toon? We wir a' pitten oot, a' da crofters fra Backa an' Brunigarth an' da idders. Da laird wantit da land fir sheep; dere's na folk livin' dere noo."

Kirstie thought of the wide firth with its gentle banks and hills, greener and less bleak than Northmavine: James' place. Harvests had been poor, the couple of years they farmed there; it was no place to lead a life of ease, but it was where she had first been a wife and run a home, where Jamie had been born. It was where she had heard the news of her father's death, like a door shutting on her childhood in Northmavine, and now it too was gone. She had a vision, for a moment, of something coming behind her, rolling up her life like a carpet.

She forced her mind back to attend to Thomas, who having found an audience was pouring out the tale of the evictions. She made the right noises of indignation and commiseration, while he rambled bitterly about men racing to get the crop out of the ground, families living in turf shelters on the moors, thatches burning on the empty crofts.

"Whin did du come ta Lerook?" she asked.

"Twartree weeks fae syne .... Kirstie, lass, whit wye can du live here?" He gestured with his shovel at the dark stone walls and the filthy pavement, his eyes desperate and trapped. "I've me aald midder ta feed; I've aye wirked, but dis ..." He jerked his head at the barrow, not looking at it; a shiver of disgust ran through him.

"Dere's no' much wark in winter," condoled Kirstie, "whin simmer comes, du'll maybe get wark on da boats, or at da road buildin'. An' if du's ill aff fir maet, or da rent, du can ask da Board fir relief."

The man seemed to draw himself more erect. "I'd no' want dat," he declared firmly. Kirstie did not press the point; she had heard many people say that before.

His fear of the town came off him like steam off a horse. She knew she had been like that once, but she couldn't recall how it had felt, not enough to help him. She could sense him slightly ill at ease with her, partly because he was ashamed to be seen at his job, but also because, though he had at first greeted her as someone from his old life, she was part of the town now, part of the alien place. He was eyeing her patched clothes, thinking, no doubt, that she had fared poorly enough in the town and so might he. When she first came to Lerwick with James, the beggars had frightened and upset her for much the same reason.

She wanted to reassure him, to tell him that even if his worst fears came true, it wouldn't be as bad as all that. People could survive more than they thought. You got used to the filth and damp of the lanes; to

106

accepting the Board's contempt and moral disapproval along with its money. Even sleeping in the streets was all right as long as you found a sheltered spot and somewhere to store the furniture. But something told her that this would not comfort him; not now at any rate; that he would not believe he might one day settle for so little, and would be horrified if he did believe it.

She tried, instead, telling him about the good side of the town; how lively it was, and the shops so handy, and doctors for his mother; you would likely have to go miles for one in Olnafirth .... But at the mere mention of the name, the fathomless bitterness swept over his face again.

"Dat wis me hame dey tuik fir da sheep. Me place, lass." He glance round at the Street. "Dis isna me place. Me place is gane." He laughed, without mirth. "Whaur does puir folk belang, eh?"

She watched as he diminished slowly down the Street, hunched behind his barrow; soon he rounded one of the many bends, and the town had swallowed him.

In the houses, and at the backs of the shops, lamps began to flicker. They gave only a faint light; the town, huddled at the edge of the grey ocean, glowed softly. From the baker's at the foot of Mounthooly Street, the smell of new bread drifted for a moment above fish and salt and the smells of the Street. She wrinkled her nose; it was a smell to sharpen hunger.

Shapes were becoming more clearly defined: a beached boat, a hen pecking on a nearby roof, a bundle in a corner which stirred restlessly in the light, then got to its feet and shuffled off, wheezing softly. A couple of gulls, on the quay, started a screaming-match about something, and a man went whistling by to his work.

More women were coming down the lanes to the well now, chatting above the creak of the windlass and the clatter of buckets being set down. She exchanged a word with this one and that; she knew most of them. The way people moved around in the lanes, you were always running into someone who'd lived on the same landing two years back; they'd minded the bairns when you were sick, maybe, or you'd kept their furniture for them while they were between rooms.

Individuals moved on all the time — she thought of Baubie on the other side of the world — but the camaraderie of the lanes women existed above and beyond individuals, changing shape as they came and went, like some primitive creature that can lose arms and grow others. There was plenty of backbiting and quarrelling in it, like the sputtering in the fire, but it kept them warm; it was what they belonged to.

A sailor lurched by, grimacing and holding his head. His clothes looked slept in; presumably he'd nodded off wherever he had been

107

drinking. He felt in his pockets, deeper and deeper, with a look of growing consternation which could not help being comic. Kirstie smiled, but she felt sorry for him: poor lads, they were so far from home, and it was all the fault of the drink .... He turned off down one of the seaward lanes, heading for his ship; she hoped he would find the captain in a good mood. The sea was quiet this morning, the grey silky pleats just beginning to shimmer in the sun.

She started back for Church Lane, shivering slightly in the morning chill. It would be one of those cold, bright winter days. That was better than the rain, which clung to your clothes and bones, and left the old buildings damp and mouldy. But she found it caught at the lungs; she would breathe shallow and carefully, because taking a deep breath in that cold was like being stabbed with a blade of ice. The walk took longer than it should have, because she was limping a little.

Back in the room, the children were awake. Peerie Kirstie had the fire going nicely and was only waiting for the water to start making tea. Kirstie, out of breath from the stairs, handed it over and sat down heavily on the old sea-chest. Johnie jumped out of bed and ran across to hug her. She cuddled him, too pleased with his spontaneous affection to mind that he'd knocked what breath she had left out of her.

Jamie was still lying in bed, staring up at the cracks on the ceiling.

"Is du no' gettin' up da day?" she asked sharply, knowing as she said it that she sounded like her mother.

"Whit fir?"

Kirstie gestured at the night-soil bucket in the corner.

"Du cud tak' dat oot."

He shrugged, and swung himself out of bed. He hadn't bothered to take off any clothes the night before, so he was not at the trouble of dressing. He took the bucket and went out, without comment.

Peerie Kirstie had the tea ready. She brought it over to her mother and Johnie on the sea-chest and the three drank it together, companionably. Kirstie eased her foot out in front of her, and Johnie asked quickly: "Is dee fit still hurtin'?"

"It's no' too bad." Going barefoot in summer, she had picked up some infection in her heel and it had never cleared up; there was an abscess which would burst every so often, so that she thought it was finished with, but it always filled up again. Johnie pointed to his sister. "Her fit's bad, too."

"Och, it's nathin'," said the girl defensively, as Kirstie checked the foot with concern. "I wasna fir bodderin' you wi it." It was, in fact, an abscess very like her mother's; it was uncanny, sometimes, how the child mirrored her.

"I'll tak dee ta Dr Cowie, later. Du'd best rest it, noo."

When Jamie came back, the girl made to get up and fetch his tea, but Kirstie waved her back and limped over to the fire. Though the tea was cooling by now, he drank it very slowly, as if he wanted it to last all morning. Kirstie had long finished hers, and had picked up the stocking she was working on.

She let her eyes rest on Johnie, who would be off to school soon; she always missed his chirpiness and ready affection. But the lass had best stay home, with her foot the way it was .... She was knitting too, almost as fast as her mother. Kirstie recalled herself and Mary, racing to finish a stocking first.

"Is du gaun oot da day?" she asked Jamie. He was finished with the school; sometimes he got casual work running errands and the like. He put the cup down.

"Aye, I suppose." He and Johnie left together; she went to the window to watch them out of sight. Johnie bounded off up Church Lane, waving as he went; Jamie strolled the other way, towards the Street. On the way, he met Elizabeth, the old widow from downstairs, coming back from the well. He passed; hesitated a moment, then turned back and carried the full bucket for her.

Kirstie stayed a long time at the window, and the child glanced up curiously; it was so unlike her mother to stand idle. The truth was, she was thinking of Thomas Anderson and his question: where do poor folk belong? In a family, she thought; among friends; if you were going to fight the system, you needed allies.

And in the place where your life had been made; poor Thomas, with that taken from him .... She tried to imagine someone wiping out Lerwick like that: the grey and bright mornings, the filth and friendship of the lanes, shops and sailors and Saturday beggars, hard winters and blazing barrels, all gone together; no, she would be as lost as Thomas without that.

The window got no morning sun; she shivered and turned back to the fire, back into the room. That was another place poor folk belonged: in a room you could heat and lock and keep your few bits and pieces safe in. She always felt she could survive most things, if she had four walls to wrap around her.

Chapter 20
Lerwick: 1854

Jerome Caddel began to think he was getting old. Work had seemed harder today, and the way home longer. There was a nagging prickle at the back of his mouth, and a shiver in his bones; he was surely catching a chill. He stopped off in Commercial Street to buy a bit of food and some whisky; maybe he could kill whatever was wrong by morning.

At the bottom of Fox Lane he rested, leaning against the wall. The thought of the steep climb took all the heart out of him; for a moment, he was not sure he could summon up the energy. What galvanised him was the sight of two children in the Street: a girl about eleven and a younger boy. They had stockings but no shoes; there was blood on one of the girl's stockings and she walked with a limp. He knew who she was; she looked very like her mother.

His lip curled with the old irritation. She stirred no feeling of possessiveness in him. She looked pallid and frail; nothing of a worker, and lame into the bargain: nearly a hundred months of one-and-fourpences. He turned away with a grunt and attacked the climb: at least he had two sound legs.

In his room he got a fire going, noting impatiently that every movement took him longer than usual. Though it was spring, and sunny outside, he could not feel warm. He sat staring at his boots for some time, working up the energy to take them off. Some young lads on the road gang that day had ribbed him about being too old for the job. Probably that had been the start of his troubles, for he had swung his pick with unreasonable vigour all day after that, to show he was a match for them; his whole body ached from it.

For a few hours he could keep that up; he still had the know-how, and the tough, sinewy frame, and above all an iron will. But in the long term he knew they were right: he was sixty-two and in a few more years he would be too old to work like that. He should start saving money, he thought, knowing that he never would. He sipped the whisky, rolling it round the back of his mouth and wishing it would warm him up. The food was on the table, but he now found he had no appetite for it.

Being ill irritated him. It was a byword with the gang that he never took a day off sick, and when anyone remarked on it, he generally replied that it was all very well for men to stay in bed who had families to fuss over them; for himself, he couldn't be bothered. He did not really doubt that he would be at work the following day. But he felt very tired. He finished the whisky and went to bed: a good sleep would put him right.

Next morning he had a headache, which at first he put down to the whisky. But as soon as he got up and started trying to move about, he knew he could never get to work. He could scarcely walk across the room without feeling exhausted, and every inch of him ached. He stumbled back to bed and slept, on and off, till noon. Then he woke with a raging thirst and realised there was no water left: he would have to go to the well. *I can't. I'll never manage that walk, and then maybe a wait in a queue. But I have to. So I will. One step. Another. Another.*

He did manage it too, though on the way back he had to haul the bucket up the stairs one at a time, and each step took minutes. He was used to making his body obey him. He forced himself to eat something too, though he still had no appetite. This was a hell of a bad chill. The headache was no better, either. *All right. Couple of days in bed. It'll go away.*

On the third day he couldn't face eating anything, nor did he bother with the fire, since it seemed to make no odds to the constant chill in him. He drank a lot of water, and the bucket was getting low again, but he told himself that when it was gone he would do without it. He was feverish and light-headed: lying in bed he found himself thinking of his mother, his wife, Kirstie and her child; they seemed to keep following each other round the room and he couldn't think why one or other of them didn't go to the well. *Just one more day. I'll be over it then.*

But the next morning he saw the fever rash all over his body. Then he knew.

The makeshift hospital at the Knab was full of typhus patients. Some had slipped into coma; others were delirious. He knew his own mind was wandering: at one point he noticed God standing by the bed and explained that he couldn't come yet because he had his work to go to. During a more lucid interval, he lay looking out of the small window, tracing patterns in a sky of cirrus clouds. The wind kept moving them out of the frame, just as he made some sense of them.

Towards evening, when the patterns were getting rather beautiful, there came a sudden tightness across his chest and upper arms. He called out, but the pain took his breath and anyway no attendant was near. So he died alone, as he had always known he would.

Dr Cowie had seen peerie Kirstie in the Street too, and scolded her mother about it.

"Why do you ask my advice, if you will not follow it? I told you that lass's foot would never get well if she walked on it; nor will yours for the matter of that. Can you no' understand: you have abscesses; it's a thing that requires rest? I'll not treat either one of you for it again; you've neither sense nor gratitude."

He turned on his heel, leaving Kirstie wondering how he thought they were to live. Did he seriously suppose they had the option of sitting in chairs all day? Of course the child's lameness worried her, far more than her own did. But if they didn't all go out to sell their work, and do what else they could find, and beg and scavenge when they had to, then there'd be no food to come home to. Henry had cut off the allowance again lately, and she was trying to make enough to pay the rent as well as feed them.

Because of the sudden cessation of the monthly one-and-fourpences, she was one of the few people who noticed that Jerome Caddel had died. Someone on the road gang remarked briefly that the old man seemed to have packed in working at last, but the first his neighbours knew was when the landlord had the room cleared out for a new tenant. Even the woman who came to clean it had almost nothing to do; as she said later, you might think it had never been lived in.

But to Kirstie the difference in income was crucial; by June she could no longer make even an attempt at paying the rent and Wlliam Hay promptly ordered them out. He tended to be wary of unpaid rent; having been bankrupt once, he had no intention of trying it again. Paupers were quite a good risk, as long as the Board was guaranteeing their rent, but any hint of an official change of mind made him nervous.

Luckily the weather was mild. Kirstie went through the usual drill; cajoling Elizabeth Twatt, the old widow who lived downstairs, to take in the furniture, and arranging to put her case to the next Board meeting. Peerie Kirstie and Johnie were inclined to make a game out of sleeping in the street: Jamie, after a couple of nights, went off to make his own arrangements, which Kirstie did not ask about. He was sixteen now, and told her even less of his thoughts. Elizabeth let them make tea, and get warm at her fire when it was raining; she was always kind.

But after the Board meeting at the end of the month, they were reinstated; Kirstie and Jamie carrying the furniture back to their old room while Johnie improvised a tune on a penny whistle. Kirstie was celebrating the triumph of optimism again.

"I telt ye it'd be a' richt an' da Board wud pay."

"Aye," said Jamie, "till da neist time. Sam Henry stops it whin he wants, nae matter whit da Board says."

"But he has ta tell dem, an' den day aye gie us da rent again. Da law's fir wis, he canna mend dat."

Jamie shrugged, but Kirstie felt buoyed up and happy, despite the cough and the stitch in her side which sleeping in the open had brought on again. She'd had that before; it would soon go away in the good weather, now they were warm at night.

Her limp did not mend much, though; nor did the little girl's. Kirstie did try to keep her home more, but she was eager to be out and about with Johnie, and wouldn't co-operate. Kirstie did not like to try Dr Cowie again. She took the girl round to Chromate Lane, where Andrew Goudie the watchmaker lived.

Aside from making watches, Goudie was a sort of amateur doctor with an interest in homoepathic remedies; more to the point, he often gave his knowledge free to his neighbours. He was a bachelor, the kind of man who has any number of acquaintances but few close friends; some people found him uncomfortably moralistic but Kirstie got on well with him. He looked at the abscesses, but shook his head.

"I canna treat these, Kirstie, ye need Cowie. Anyway I shudna take his patients."

"He wudna help; he said we'd ta rest da feet or he'd no' treat dem."

"Well he's right, ye shud. But it's no' always easy, I ken. I'm glad ye're back in a room."

"I wis thankfu' ta ye, whin we wir oot o' it." Andrew had given her money now and then, when she had no roof and could not knit.

"Och, it's no matter. How's your neighbours that used to live up the closs from me?"

Kirstie grimaced. "Da auld man disna get oot much. But I canna laek Keetie fir a neebir. She quarrels wi' aabody, whin she's drink in her."

"Well, she's had a hard life too, ye know. But it's a shame about the drink, right enough." Andrew was a leading light in the Lerwick Total Abstinence Society; one of the reasons he and Kirstie got on was that he approved of her aversion to drink.

That October, Samuel Henry found himself in the bad books of the Supervision Board in Edinburgh, once again. Charles Gilbert Duncan had sent a written request for him to do something about a woman called Williamson, who according to Duncan was supposed to be starving, and he hadn't got around to it. Henry read the correspondence with his usual irritation, wondering how much of it he needed to trouble his own Board with.

The October meeting was coming up, when he must present the up-to-date Roll of Paupers for their consideration. The rent day of Martinmas was just around the corner; they would be wanting to see if anyone's circumstances had changed, and indeed if any general policy change was needed. Personally he reckoned he could make a good case for revising all the allowances downwards, if they would listen to him.

They often didn't, which was one of the things he found really irksome about the Inspector's job. He was no civil servant by nature, as Burns had been; he wanted to make policy, not carry out someone else's. But he had one great advantage over Burns: he was also the secretary, who reported to the Board and wrote its minutes. The Board could only interfere with his decisions if and when it knew about them, and for some time now he had been acting first and notifying the Board later, often months later. They could still overrule him then, but often it was easier to let matters stand.

And when they made the wrong decision, or with the wrong emphasis, he could sometimes give it a different slant in the minutes. They were all busy men, for whom the Board was a fraction of their time, and few people remember from month to month exactly what was said at a meeting. (He himself had almost word-for-word recall of such things, but then he genuinely liked being a secretary.)

The June minutes on Christina Inkster, for instance. All it said on the page was "payment of rent to be continued till Martinmas." Well he knew what that meant; the Board had resolved the same thing God knew how many times; it meant that at the meeting before Martinmas, they would review the case and decide if the allowance was still justified.

But the minutes didn't actually say so. If he read them literally, he could consider himself authorised to discontinue it again, and strike her off the Roll. If any Board member noticed her absence from that, there would likely be a debate, which he would doubtless lose yet again, but it was highly improbable: out of sight, out of mind. She would get herself back on eventually, no doubt; she always seemed to be able to get around somebody: still, he could save the ratepayers' money for a month or so.

So far, he was only doing what he had done many times before; the resumption of normal hostilities, really. But he then took his pen to write a letter to William Hay, and that was different. *It will be distinctly understood that all my obligations for the rent of rooms occupied by poor people are at an end and cease at Martinmas.* He paused, then added, with an artistic hyphen, *the allowances to all of them being reduced.* After all, he was going to put the idea of the reduction to the next meeting, and if they'd any sense, they would agree to it.

He added his characteristic, beautiful signature. As a specimen of handwriting, the whole letter was beautiful, as all his letters were.

PART SIX

"IT IS NOTHING TO YOU"

Chapter 21
Lerwick: November-December, 1854

Testimony of James Jamieson to Charles Gilbert Duncan. Procurator Fiscal of Shetland

I am the eldest child of Christina Inkster or Jamieson sometimes called Kirstie Caddel. My father died when I was little more than a year old .... Sometime prior to Martinmas last we lived in a room in Church Lane and my mother partly supported herself and us by knitting and partly by assistance received from charitable people. She also occasionally got trifling sums from Mr Samuel Henry, Inspector of Poor. A few days after the term of Martinmas last we were turned out of the room by a Sheriff Officer and our things put out into the close.

Peerie Kirstie and young Johnie perched on the bed, huddling together under the covers. They were not particularly worried: after all, the furniture had been out in the lane in June, and that hadn't lasted long. It was a lot colder now, though, and they hoped things would be sorted out soon. They tried to joke with Jamie, but he sat silently on the old sea-chest, biting his nails. He was the only one who actually recalled sleeping in the street in the winter of 1846.

Kirstie was upstairs in the house, trying to persuade the new tenant to keep the furniture for them till they got a room again. Presently she called down to Jamie, and he began carrying a few things back upstairs. Thomas Tulloch, the new man, accepted a couple of chairs and smaller items but drew the line at the chest and bed. Kirstie and Jamie rejoined the children.

"Whit'll we do noo?" asked Jamie, with no interest or hope in his voice.

"I'll see Henry. Da Board's bound ta pay da room rent."

Jamie shrugged, but Kirstie began limping determinedly up the road, towards Henry's office in the Subscription Rooms. But she had hardly started when she saw James Wilson, the police superintendent, coming from the Rooms, and realised to her surprise that he was making for her and the children. She stopped, and he came down to them and stood looking at the pair on the bed.

"Whit way is da Board no' paid da rent again, Mr Wilson? Dey said dey still wid."

"I widna ken, Kirstie, it's the lass I'm come for. The Board 'll still pay her room, her being a cripple, and they've gotten a place for her."

Kirstie put her arm around the child. "Wha'll tak her? Elspet?"

"No." Wilson shifted from one foot to another and did not meet her eye. "Mr Henry's told me to tak her to Katie Laing's."

"What? Drunken Keetie? No! I'll no' have dat!"

"Weel dan, come and tell Henry you dunna laek it; he wants me to fetch ye anyway. But I hae ta tak the lass, Kirstie, I canna do idder."

They clung to each other, crying, their dark hair tangled together. The child limped very badly now, he noticed; he had to help her up the stairs to Laing's.

Testimony of James Wilson, Superintendent of Police

I placed the child in Laing's room much against her own will and left her crying. The mother was also crying and I took her to Mr Henry.

"Why Keetie?" Kirstie kept repeating as they walked up the lane. Wilson thought she might well ask. Of course he was aware the two women were on the worst of terms. But then, so was Henry.

The Inspector was looking his most imposing when they entered, but to Wilson's surprise she went straight on to the attack, demanding bitterly what he thought he was doing, placing a child with that woman, instead of paying the rent in the first place and keeping them together. Henry was taken aback, Wilson noted with some satisfaction. But he rallied quickly.

"Such matters are for me to decide. I have placed the child where I judge she will be best off, and if you interfere you will be taken to court, and very likely to prison. I have had you fetched here for the Superintendent to caution you to that effect, so that you cannot claim not to have understood it."

He nodded to Wilson, who went through the caution, wooden-faced. He was furious with Henry for putting him in this position, when there were any number of women the child could have been sent to, without causing all this fuss. When she left, he managed to slip out and have a quick word.

"Dinna defy him, Kirstie, ye'll maybe end up in the jail and ye've the peerie lad to think of, too."

She nodded; she had evidently been working things out for herself. "I'll go ta da Board meetin' an' tell dem how it is. Den dey'll pay da rent again."

Well they would probably tell Henry to, thought Wilson; the question was whether he would listen. He had been taken aback by Henry's obvious animosity to the woman; she had always struck him as a peaceable type, except where her children were concerned.

118

Back in the lane, she hung about outside the house, her eyes fixed on Laing's window. Once the child's face appeared, looking up and down the lane, but someone pulled her away. Kirstie called, but could not tell if the girl had heard or seen her. She bit her nails, already short and broken with work, as far down as she could. Damn Henry; why must he keep doing this? It wouldn't have worried her so much normally, apart from being the wrong time of year, but she could not leave a child with that woman; they would have to get a room again quickly, where they could be back together.

She took the boys down to the Street, to take her mind off peerie Kirstie. She still had a little knitting to sell; another reason to sort the Board out quickly, for without a room she could do no work. But the loss of the child had thrown her off balance; she could not think straight, and to the boys' questions about what they would do, she merely replied that she would see in the morning.

When the light began to fail, they returned to the lane. Jamie and Johnie, sitting on the bed, looked expectantly up, waiting for her to decide what to do next.

The west wind was biting; Johnie was shivering under the covers. She made up her mind quickly; they could not sleep in the lane, not in winter. She motioned them off the bed, and began to lift the mattress.

"Help me get it up da stairs, Jamie, we'll put it on da stairheid. Johnie, bring da covers."

The landing at the top of the first flight was about six feet wide; they managed to wedge the thing in next to what had been their room, and was now Thomas Tulloch's. It took up almost the whole landing between his door and William Simpson's opposite. Here they were less exposed than in the lane, but not by much; it was unfortunate that the open entrance-way faced the west wind. They slept fitfully, huddling for warmth, waking often and turning back to back, trying to get all of themselves warm at once.

They had not been there long when they heard footsteps on the stairs. At first, Kirstie thought it was someone coming home late, and hoped it was neither Tulloch nor William Simpson, both of whom would have to step over them. But then she thought she knew the halting step, clattering unevenly on the stone steps, and told herself she was just imagining it.

The covers lifted, and peerie Kirstie slid in beside her mother. From the flurry of whispered questions it emerged that Katie Laing had at first taken matters very seriously, assuring the girl that she would never see her mother again. During the afternoon, however, her interest in fostering had tailed off markedly; peerie Kirstie had managed to get back outside and had been waiting for the safety of darkness to rejoin them.

119

Kirstie supposed she should worry about the police caution. But after all, she hadn't interfered herself. She hugged the child closer; they whispered and giggled in the dark like a pair of sisters.

In the morning, the creak of Tulloch's door opening woke them. Kirstie blinked up into his startled eyes.

"It's just till da Board finns wis a room; it'll no' be lang." He smiled and nodded.

Elizabeth downstairs let them make tea at her fire. The children, stiff from a night's cold, thawed out luxuriously, while Kirstie took stock. She could think better, now; it seemed obvious what must be done and she couldn't imagine why she had been so much at a loss.

There was a Parochial Board meeting due at the end of the month, to which she could go and explain her circumstances. But that was still about ten days off. It wasn't just the cold at nights; what mattered far more was the not being able to do any knitting. That meant she could not feed the children. She sent Jamie off to Henry to ask for a weekly allowance until they got a room again; the standard procedure. Then she went up the lane to number 14 and talked Margaret Cheyne into letting peerie Kirstie sleep by her fire until the meeting. The girl stopped behind at Cheyne's, playing with Margaret's new baby.

As they walked back towards the Street, Kirstie glanced down at Johnie.

"I cud finn dee a place, as weel. Elspet's, maybe?"

He shook his head, and gave her his friendly grin. "Na, I'll bide wi you."

They went into the Street, their arms around each other, to see what they could beg.

Near the harbour they met Jamie, begging on his own account; he had been trying to pick up some casual work and failing, mainly because his clothes were so tattered. He had done better at the begging, though, and shared a hunk of bread with them. When she caught sight of him first, Kirstie had seen, as a stranger might, how damp and rumpled his clothes looked, how thin he was, and how the dark eyes stared out of his pallid face. She could see why he couldn't get a job.

"Is du gotten onything frae Henry?"

He shook his head impatiently. "Just his door in me face, sam as I telt ye I wid."

"Whin I tell da Board, dey'll help wis." He laughed shortly, and told her she was dreaming. He did not stay on the stairhead that night; she and Johnie kept warm alone, as best they could.

Even when she came back from the meeting, triumphantly waving the Board's guarantee of rent for the next quarter (which the reluctant Henry had been instructed to sign on the spot), Jamie was unimpressed.

"It's no' a room, is it? Or maet?"

120

"We'll finn a room sune enyoch, noo."

But it did not prove so easy. Kirstie tramped the whole of Church Lane, and all the neighbouring lanes, in the next couple of weeks, but there wasn't a house with a room vacant. She had never realised before how crowded Lerwick was these days. Before long, Yule would be approaching, and even more people flocking in to visit relatives. She began to feel a prickle of worry.

Testimony of Margaret Cheyne, housewife

So long as she had a room she used to knit and was of very active habits, but after she was put out of her room she had no means of doing any work. She seemed much troubled in her mind after being put out ....

Chapter 22
Lerwick: December, 1854

"Kirstie, I'm sorry, I wiss we cud keep da bairn till ye got a room, but we canna: we're poor wirsells."

"Aye, I ken dat. I'm richt grateful, Margaret."

Peerie Kirstie could still hardly walk. Her mother helped her up to the stairhead and left her on the mattress. Then she went down to the Street to sell the bedclothes.

When Jamie heard about that, he flared up for once and asked how the hell were they to keep warm.

"I had ta get maet."

"Why didna ye sell da furniture, for God's sake?"

"We'll need dat, whin we get a room again." He threw up his hands and laughed. Thomas Tulloch's door, that had once been theirs, opened and they moved aside to let him step over the mattress. Kirstie gave him good day, and he answered her kindly enough, but wrinkled his nose as he passed.

Kirstie went up the lane to see Henry herself, thinking that maybe Jamie just hadn't tried hard enough. She found the Inspector not aggressive; just curiously offhand: he leaned back in his chair and told her blandly that apart from guaranteeing the rent, he had no obligation to her. She left, feeling baffled. She knew the system far too well to suppose that was true. If you were on the roll, and the Board had guaranteed your rent, they would also pay you an interim allowance while you were between rooms. At least they always had, up to now. Had they changed the game, when she wasn't looking? Henry seemed to be playing by new rules, and she was not sure what to do about it.

Still, there was always a good side: at least he hadn't mentioned taking peerie Kirstie away this time. She was still perched on the stairhead, resting her foot. Kirstie called in to check up on her, then took Johnie down to the Street.

It was mid-December. People who were out wanted to be in; they walked quickly, not stopping to look to right or left, so muffled in collars and scarves that you could scarcely make out their faces. It was hard to get much out of folk who could barely see you, and had every good reason for hurrying on. But there was nothing for it but begging, as long as she could not work. She glanced down at Johnie; noticing her worried look, he pulled a comical face. She laughed, and caught quickly at her left side.

The sky had been grey for some time, ominously heavy and full. Preoccupied with Henry and the room, she had not noticed the weather. Suddenly, quite silently, the greyness opened and spilled, as if the old tales of a goddess in heaven shaking out her feather bed were really true. It began to snow in big, soft, swirling flakes, blotting out the passing people: new come oot o Paradise, Kirstie thought bitterly. This was serious; she and Johnie had worn out their last stockings, and as far as she could remember, the other two were no better off. Hardened as they all were to going barefoot, they could not go far in snow.

They went back to where peerie Kirstie was sitting on the mattress, wrapped in the thin counterpane which was all the covering they had left. Her stockings had no feet worth speaking of either, but even if they had, she could walk no distance.

Jamie came back soon after. He was barefoot too, but he had some tea. Kirstie perked up at the mere thought of it. They took it down to Elizabeth Twatt's, and she let them make it at her fire, looking on with concern as Johnie stared into the heart of the flames, entrancing himself with warmth.

Tea always stimulated Kirstie's mind; now another expedient occurred to her. She sent Jamie to Henry's office with the note he had signed guaranteeing their rent: maybe, since it was of no present use to them, he would exchange it for cash. After all, she had lived all her life with a system of barter.

Testimony of James Jamieson

I went to Mr Henry to return the line he had given her for her room rent and to ask for some supply. I saw his son Laurence who is a clerk in his office and told him my errand. He bade me take back the line, but I said we could not live upon the line and I laid it down on the counter and I left it.

She had sold nearly everything by now. There was a sheet and counterpane left, and a small white basin which came in handy for whatever they could beg, and a couple of chairs still at Thomas Tulloch's, which she didn't tell Jamie about. She still believed they would get another room to put furniture in, eventually: you had to go on believing that.

The snow refused to let up. But sometimes Kirstie and the boys had no option but to go out begging, whatever the weather. Usually they split up, Jamie taking Johnie with him to beg in the Street, while Kirstie looked for a room, or tried Henry and anyone else she could think of, and peerie Kirstie stayed on the stairhead, quietly noting the mounting frustration of the Tullochs and Simpsons as they stepped over her.

Andrew Goudie saw them now and then. He would not treat the two Kirsties for their foot abscesses, which he felt were beyond him, but he gave them food and tried to find a room for them, without success. Looking down at them, shivering on the increasingly disreputable mattress, he had an uncomfortable feeling that it might be his Christian duty to take them in himself ... But he was a bachelor, after all, and she a woman with two illegitimate children ... no, he couldn't be meant to do that. But he still felt uneasy enough to go and berate Henry.

Testimony of Andrew Goudie, watchmaker and homoeopath

I represented very strongly to Mr Henry the circumstances in which Inkster and her family were as I considered it a disgrace to the place that they should be left lying on a stair head and that in my opinion no long time would elapse before one or more of them would fall victims to the exposure.

On 20th December Elizabeth Twatt heard the children's voices, sounding anxious, on the stairhead. She climbed up and saw Kirstie lying on the mattress, with Johnie and peerie Kirstie beside her. She was white-faced and breathing gingerly, clutching the side where she was always complaining of pain these days.

"Come in by da fire an' get a warm", Elizabeth said hospitably, but Kirstie shook her head and turned over on the mattress. She was shivering with cold, but apparently could not face moving even to get warm. She gestured at the children to go with Elizabeth, but they stayed by her.

She lay on the stairhead all day. William Simpson came out sometimes to see her, trying to hold his breath against the worsening smell of the mattress. Once, coming back in from his shopping, (he was a widower), he showed her a lump of uncooked oatmeal.

"I'll just away an' get dis baked fir dee, Kirstie."

"Na," she said, raising herself painfully, "it'll be fine da wye it is." He gave her the tasteless stuff, surprised, and she tore at it, cramming it into her mouth faster than she could gulp it down. William watched in horrified fascination; she put him in mind of the gulls diving on the harbour scraps. He had had no idea that she had become as hungry as that; when she complained, it was almost always about the cold. It surprised him that a dying woman, which he reckoned she was, could have such a ravenous appetite.

He fed peerie Kirstie and Johnie too, in a more orthodox fashion. They were hungry, but nowhere near as bad as that; he guessed she must have been giving them most of what she got. They were both anxious and upset about her condition, and for once she seemed unable to make the effort to reassure them. Of Jamie there was no sign; there were days, now, when he hardly appeared on the stairhead.

William slipped downstairs to Elizabeth's room.

"Whit'll become o' da bairns, if she dees ida nicht?"

The old widow's face creased in pity. "Dey can come here, until da Board finns dem a place. Dey didna want ta leave her, an' dey shud be dere, if she's deein '."

"Och, she'll be deid by mornin', dat's shure."

A pause fell between them, because neither wished to admit that their first reaction to that news was relief. They had nothing to say against her, except that she was poor and sick and hungry and lying outside their doors; they felt mean for resenting her. But William was coming to hate the sight of that mattress, and the smell of it which penetrated his room even with the door shut; while Elizabeth was growing as unhappy as only a kind person can be, watching suffering and being unable to stop it. They took refuge in indignation.

"It's no' richt, a body bein' left ta dee on a stairheid laek yon."

"Na, it isna. Dey shud tak' her somewye fittin '."

When William went back upstairs, Elizabeth thought some more, and then went up the road to tell Henry about it.

Testimony of Elizabeth Twatt, widow

He said: you have no business with it; it is nothing to you. I said it was my business, as she was lying at the stair head dying of cold, and it was an awful thing for her to die of hunger too.

Elizabeth and William both slept badly, half-waiting every moment to hear the children's wails from the stairhead which would announce that it was over. William was worried too about the candle-ends he had left with them; part of him felt they ought not to be in darkness, but the more prudent part wondered if the mattress would not catch alight and set fire to the house. At least its dampness should be some protection.

Next morning Elizabeth woke with a start, as if there were something urgent to be doing. She was puzzled a moment, then remembered and listened. Upstairs she could hear a hollow cough, and quiet voices, trying not to wake anyone. She slipped up to the stairhead.

To her utter amazement, Kirstie was up and doing. The cough had come from Johnie, who looked to have a bad cold; he was lying on the mattress and his mother was giving him water from the little white basin.

"Why, lass, is du better?"

Kirstie straightened, catching her side. "Aye, weel enyoch. It's da boy, he canna stay oot here ida caald. I'll hae ta mak' Henry finn him a place."

Elizabeth could only shake her head in half-reluctant, baffled admiration. Kirstie was plainly still very unwell; it must have taken a terrific effort of will just to get up, but there it was: as soon as one of the

125

children needed her she could force it from somewhere. Elizabeth wondered if there were anything she could not bounce back from.

The door across the landing opened, and William Simpson looked out. His face met Elizabeth's, and she read the mirror of her own feelings — astonishment, and respect, and a guilty lack of gladness.

Chapter 23
Lerwick: 20th December, 1854
— 9th January, 1855

Kirstie managed to drag herself to the well to get more water for Johnie, but she could not face the uphill walk to Henry's office. As soon as Jamie came back, she sent him, with instructions to demand that Henry pay someone to house and feed the child while he was ill.

When she saw James Wilson coming up the stair, she backed Johnie into a corner and stood in front of him.

"Dunna fret, lass," said the superintendent, "aye, I'm meant to tak' him to Laing's, but I'm no' planning on it."

He had in fact come very close to telling Henry to pursue his feud himself, until he reflected that there was a simpler way. He did take the boy to Katie's door, where he mentioned casually that the symptoms looked not unlike typhus fever to him. Even in the course of police work, he had seldom had a door slammed in his face faster. Then he took him down to Elizabeth Twatt's.

In the lanes, a stench had to be something spectacular to be noticed above the common run. In the case of the mattress and its occupants, it was composed of long-standing damp, sickness, clothes not changed for a month, stuff brought in on people's feet, and a couple of times Johnie hadn't managed to get out to the lane soon enough. Thomas Tulloch had got into the habit of taking an enormous stride as he left his front door, so as not to step on it.

Neither the Tullochs nor the Simpsons could go in or out without stepping over the mattress and whoever was on it at the time. Katie Laing was complaining of the smell more bitterly every day, and even Elizabeth, downstairs, was conscious of it. Kirstie came in often to see Johnie. The sight of her was beginning to terrify Elizabeth. She was gaunt, her face white, with the great dark eyes staring out and the skin drawn taut over the bones; dressed in whatever she could find to throw on. Her breath rasped; she complained constantly of pain and even by the fire she hugged herself and shivered. Long after she had left, the sour odour would hang in the room: to Elizabeth it seemed that if suffering itself had a smell, it would be just like this.

Whatever was wrong with Johnie, warmth and food put right in a few days. He announced one morning, quite chirpily, that he was fine and well now and would go upstairs to his mother again. Elizabeth was concerned, but did not try to stop him. On the stair he passed Thomas Tulloch, who had just tripped over the mattress for the umpteenth time.

Samuel Henry, in his office at the top of the lane, was emphatically in a Town Clerk mood. It was the thirtieth of December: Yule was coming close, and his annual battle with the forces of disorder. There were pleasanter prospects too; his friends and children had parties planned, and there would be fine singing in the Kirk... He hummed under his breath, in his deep, melodious voice. Added to which, he was trying to compose a loyal address to the Crown, on the subject of the war in the Crimea.

He was not, therefore, best pleased to be accosted yet again about Kirstie. Thomas Tulloch was the latest in what seemed a never-ending procession of people wishing to bother themselves and him with her. She herself had not been for a while, but he saw her begging in the Street sometimes, and the needier she looked, the more he resented her.

Testimony of Thomas Tulloch, neighbour

I told him she could not be allowed to lie any longer on the stairhead. Mr Henry replied that I might make of her what I liked.

Kirstie knew there must be another Board meeting due soon, but she had lost faith in it. What was the use of their ordering Henry to relieve her, if he ignored them? She had not given up, though. Jamie had brought some food back, and as soon as she felt stronger she went seeking help in the other direction, to the old Tolbooth at the bottom of the lane. It had been the town jail once, before Fort Charlotte, but they called it the town house, these days; the post office was there, and the Sheriff's office. Before now, the Sheriff Court had issued orders to Henry to relieve her; maybe he had to pay more heed to them. She still could not work out how he had managed to change the rules; but she had always had faith in the law.

The Sheriff listened, and promised to look into it. At lunchtime, running into Henry in the Street, he brought the matter up casually. And Henry replied: och, it was all lies; the woman had a guarantee of rent and he himself had offered her help, which she'd refused. So when she came back in the afternoon, the Sheriff turned her away.

This came as near as anything to shattering her. The law had never failed her before; now it was as if someone had cut off access to it. She went back the next day, to try to speak to the Sheriff again, but only his clerk was in. He was sympathetic, and gave her a penny for food, but held out no hope.

Jamie laughed shortly when she told him.

"Whit wis du expectin'? Da law's nae help for folk laek wis. Naethin' is."

"Weel," she said, "we got da penny. An' Yule E'en's sune comin'; dat'll be a gude nicht ta beg. Folk's aye kind den."

They duly went out, into the light of candles and flames, the noise of firecrackers, and the reek of gunpowder and tar. Even in her state of health, just being in all that light revived her. Actually people were not all that generous; they had come out to enjoy themselves, not to be reminded of other folk's misery. But there was a fair amount to be scavenged from the ground; little Johnie was particularly adept at that. Kirstie thought they had done quite well.

But she caught a bad cold, being out so late, and could not shake it off. After three or four days of it, Jamie became so alarmed that he went to see Henry, little as he hoped from him.

Testimony of James Jamieson

Mr Henry was very angry and said he had nothing to do with her.

On the eighth of January, Kirstie again felt unable to leave the mattress. They tried to ration what they begged, but they were always so hungry that they generally failed. From what they had got the day before, she had managed to keep back a raw turnip. She shared it between Johnie and peerie Kirstie — Jamie was off somewhere fending for himself. Peerie Kirstie was almost a fixture on the mattress now; she could hardly hobble. She tried to get her mother to share the turnip, but Kirstie refused: "I'm no' hungered, lass." She would have told the girl that anyway, but curiously enough it was true; she hadn't felt hungry for a few days, which at least was a mercy. Peerie Kirstie glanced anxiously at her.

Long-distance diagnosis from Dr John Cowie

Four or five days ago her little daughter called and asked me to come and see her mother. I refused to go, believing that her object was to obtain pecuniary and not medical assistance.

Next day there was no food. Jamie was still away; he might bring back food for them, but she could not bank on it. Peerie Kirstie, after her trek to the doctor, wasn't fit to walk down the lane, and Kirstie would not send little Johnie alone. So she got up again, because she had to.

She picked up almost the only thing still left lying beside the mattress, the small white basin, and she and Johnie went down to the Street, leaving peerie Kirstie on the mattress.

After a few minutes, Katie Laing went down the stairs, casting a malevolent glance at the mattress as she passed. Peerie Kirstie heard her knock on Elizabeth Twatt's door and go in. About ten more minutes went by.

129

Katie came upstairs again, clattering; she was carrying a mop and bucket. Elizabeth followed, with cleaning rags and some soap.

"Geeng aff an' play, du," said Katie, "we're gaun ta redd up da stairheid."

She spoke, for her, almost amicably, and peerie Kirstie was at once on guard, glancing warily at Elizabeth.

"Aye, we'll sune be done," confirmed the old widow, not looking directly at her, "du can come back in a while an' it'll be grand an' clean."

Testimony of Elizabeth Twatt. widow

On Tuesday she went out, and I and Catherine Laing put her bedding on top of an old chest of hers outside the house as the smell had become so offensive.

Jamie came back first, in the early afternoon, and saw the mattress draped clumsily over the sea-chest. Peerie Kirstie, the tatty counterpane wrapped around her, sat on the ground beside it. He took it all in at a glance, and nodded.

"I tocht dey'd no' be long."

"Is du gotten onything?"

He shook his head, and spread his palms wide. "Da Street wis nae gude, da day. I'll try da docks, later." He sat down beside her, to wait for his mother.

She came about four, limping round the corner from the Street with Johnie trailing after her. He was very tired, but when he saw his brother and sister he perked up: "Mammy sold da basin, look." He pointed to a couple of bread rolls in Kirstie's hand.

She looked at the mattress, and the other two. Peeerie Kirstie spoke up: "Elspet an' Katie pat it oot."

Jamie jerked his thumb at the stair: "Will I carry it back up?"

The light was going, but there was still enough to see the mattress by; more than there had been on the stairhead. She gazed in fascinated disgust at the stained, filthy thing which looked so much worse out in the light of day. A sudden keen memory assailed her; the smell of clothes drying in the salty wind off the voe.

She turned her eyes to Hay's building, where they had lived four years; where she knew everybody. Its grimy frontage was a block of deeper darkness in the twilight; behind the windows no lights could yet be seen. It looked edgy; unwelcoming.

"Na," she said, "na, we canna go back."

They moved the mattress off and sat down on the chest; she split the rolls among the children. They ate them slowly, carefully, not missing a crumb. Then they sat in silence for a while, as it grew darker, till Jamie asked: "Whit' ll we dae?"

130

Kirstie had thought of that by now: they would go to the old Tolbooth. The front door was open late; they could sneak up the stair and find some corner.

They gathered up the tattered sheet and counterpane. In the open air, Kirstie could hardly bear to smell the things, but they had no other covering. They set off down the lane, going slowly on account of peerie Kirstie's limp.

The child was wearing part of an old sheet as a petticoat, and the boys were in an ill-fitting assortment of old clothes. They walked a little warily, as barefoot folk do, huddling against the wind. Kirstie contemplated them and herself with wonder, almost a lack of recognition. *How did we get to this?*

They looked patient, hopeless, needy: a terrifying sight. As they turned the corner out of the lane, Hay's building seemed to breathe out with relief.

Chapter 24
Lerwick: 9th-11th January, 1855

There was plenty of traffic at the Town House, but the Sheriff's Clerks and post office staff affected not to see them, and they found a corner on the stairhead. They had hoped to creep into a room, but those not in use were all locked. As the various offices closed, the clerks locked them too, before leaving.

Behind them on the stairhead was a broken window, with the wind whipping through it.

"God," muttered Jamie through chattering teeth, "dis is caalder den da idder place. I'm gaun oot ta beg."

"I'll ging, too," volunteered Johnie.

"No," Jamie replied abruptly. He did take Johnie sometimes, when he begged in the Street; the child's engaging face was a help. But he was not planning on going to the Street.

While he was gone, Kirstie examined the other proceeds from the sale of the basin, a screw of tea, and wondered where she could get some water boiled. Margaret would let her, but she didn't think she could move again tonight. Maybe Jamie would go, when he got back. It was dark on the stairhead; they had no candle-ends left. There was no moon to speak of, either; now and again stars were visible through the broken pane, but the wind kept blowing cloud over them.

Jamie was some time gone; when he returned he handed over two ship's biscuits.

"Whaur are dey frae?"

"Sailors, on da *Janet Hay*." He sat staring into the dark, and did not seem disposed to talk. She halved and shared out the biscuits, glancing sadly at his pale, morose face; he would be handsome, if he didn't look so old for sixteen.

His silence inhibited her; it was a while before she felt able to ask him to go to Margaret 's. She could hardly see him now; he was just a shape in the dark. She added: "See if du can get a bit o' candle."

He reached for the tea and set off, but called back from the foot of the stair: "Dey're locked da door fir da nicht."

She sighed, and settled down with the children, but thirst kept her awake. She felt fevered and hot.

On the Wednesday, though, she woke cold even to the touch. Jamie went to try Dr Cowie again. While he was gone, Johnie and peerie Kirstie went out on the Street for a quiet scavenge and found a bootlace.

"We cud sell it ta someane an' get maet," suggested the ever-optimistic Johnie. They tried with various passers-by, but could find no takers. In the end, dispirited, they collected the tea from Kirstie and went up Church Lane, to Margaret Cheyne's house.

Margaret listened with concern, and gave them a halfpenny for the bootlace. They lingered by the fire, playing with the baby, while she boiled water for the tea.

The stairhead Kirstie was lying on led to the belfry; it was not much frequented and those people who saw her merely glanced curiously for a moment and turned their minds to their own affairs. She lay and listened to the folk calling at the post office, inquiring after their letters: in the Sheriff's office, she could hear the young clerk humming a reel tune which she knew from somewhere but could not place. Her head felt light and it was an effort to sit up.

Through the broken window came the noise of gulls; through the front door, the sounds of the Street. Boots echoing on the pavement, a snort from one of the little peat-carrying ponies, two women in a shrill quarrel. It was all just as usual, without her; it was chilling to realise that things would still go on just as usual if she were not there at all. For the first time ever, she felt a wave of bitterness against the town for its lack of need of her, of any individual. James could die, and Magnus, and she herself, and it would go blithely on its way without noticing. *How could I make so little difference?*

Johnie and peerie Kirstie came back in high glee, having bought a roll with the halfpenny. They split some off and gave it to Kirstie. Seeing them concerned, she tried to get it down, but almost at once she shook her head. She sipped the tea instead, and watched them eat.

Jamie came partway up the stairs. "I guidt ta Cowie. He'll no' treat ony paupers without a line frae Henry, ta say da Board 'll pay him his money. An' I canna get one. He wasna at da Subscription Rooms, just dat son o' his dat wirks fir him, an' he said he cudna help."

Kirstie nodded. "Aa weel, it's nae matter. I'll no' be needin' Cowie. Are ye comin' up?"

"Na. I'll no' bide anidder nicht in here. I'll find somewhere." He turned and left.

By the Thursday, quite a few neighbours had got to know where she was; she had a blurred impression of people trooping in and out with things. Elizabeth came, and Margaret with coffee and a hot stone for her feet: that was welcome, for she could hardly feel them. Margaret touched them, and resolved to come back later with a pair of stockings. But the best was the flicker of the few candle-ends. She knew they

133

should go easy on them, save them against need, but she couldn't. More than warmth, or food, or medicine, or even a roof, she wanted light; she felt that if the whole stairhead blazed with candles, it would scarcely be enough.

Jamie turned up too, at some point, and took Johnie out begging with him, and then later they came back with some bread and she tried to eat, but nothing would go down ... She felt herself drifting on the edge of sleep.

Testimony of Margaret Cheyne

About seven that evening I heard the girl's voice calling out for somebody to come with a light as her mother was dead. I could not leave the house at that moment, as there was no one at home to look after my young child, but some of the neighbours went down with a light, and found she had only fainted. When my husband came home at 8p.m. I went down to the Town House and found her lying upon the inner stairhead on a little straw. The crippled girl had a candle in her hand.

Gideon Blance from over the road was there; a soft, impressionable sort of man, trying unsuccessfully to get her to eat some biscuits. It seemed she could not swallow anything solid. She was conscious, though. He asked if she wanted a doctor.

"Look at dat lass's fit," she replied bitterly, "whit use wis he tae her?"

Some other neighbour muttered that it was a scandal folk were let get into this state.

"Aye, weel," Blance said mildly, "it's da will o' God, I suppose."

The woman on the straw seemed to wake more fully. In a much more powerful voice, she said: "It's frae men I'm sufferin' dis, an' no' frae God."

She struggled slightly more upright, and looked around for the children.

"Come an' shak hands, I'm dyin'."

Blance, who was beginning to find the whole thing upsetting, slipped out. So did Margaret, to fetch Andrew Goudie. And so, after a little while, did Jamie.

Andrew Goudie came at once: took a look at her and went off at a run for Henry.

Testimony of Samuel Henry. Inspector of Poor

We found her lying on the stair head with her two youngest children beside her, crying. I asked her what was the matter with her. I observed some biscuit and loaf lying beside her as well as some tea and sugar and I remarked to a woman beside her that she did not appear to be ill off. It did not occur to me to send for

Dr Cowie as Mr Goudie remarked she was dying, and I made such arrangements as I thought would be necessary in the event of her death.

Post-mortem report by Dr John Cowie

The left lung was adherent to the ribs throughout the whole extent of its lateral and anterior surface: the adhesions were strong and apparently of long standing. The lung was still pervious to the air although its usefulness would have been much impaired.

The stomach seemed to be perfectly healthy and contained 3-4 oz of fluid which appeared to be water gruel. This fluid contained some small portions of what appeared to be leaves of tea and a few black specks, apparently ground coffee. The small intestine contained a small quantity of chyme. The large intestine was empty.

The scalp over the back of the head was strongly adherent to the cranium and on separating it a quantity of serum flowed. It is stated by medical authorities that effusion of serum in the cavities of the brain sometimes results from an injurious degree of cold.

Testimony of James Jamieson

Elizabeth Twatt, who had formerly been a neighbour of ours, desired my brother and sister and myself to come to her room where we still remain. She has given us food and treated us kindly.

Parochial Board relief to which Christina Inkster was entitled between mid-November 1854 and 11th January 1855

9s per quarter for 8 weeks   ca 5s 6d

Money actually disbursed by Samuel Henry to Christina Inkster during that period: None

Money disbursed by Samuel Henry in connection with Christina Inkster's death

To coffin	10s 6d
To Elizabeth Twatt, for watching by corpse	2s
To William Simpson, ditto	2s
To candles	1s 9d
	16s 3d

Epilogue

Charles Gilbert Duncan, the Procurator Fiscal, had ordered the post-mortem, on Friday, 12th January, the day after Kirstie's death. By the Saturday, he had convened a preliminary inquiry into her death and was hearing witnesses. They included two of her children, neighbours, Dr Cowie, James Wilson the police superintendent, Samuel Henry himself and others. Many of their statements have been quoted in the preceding chapters.

Henry could scarcely deny that he had failed to afford her relief (he did have a half-hearted try, but the evidence of the procession of people who had been turned from his door left no real room for doubt.) He therefore tried to prove that she was not a "fit object of relief" for the Board, mainly by alleging that had he given her money, she would have spent it on whisky. He added for good measure that he had frequently seen her drunk about the streets. A number of solid citizens, including the superintendent of police and the secretary of the Lerwick Total Abstinence Society (Andrew Goudie) then testified the exact opposite, namely that the deceased had been of notably sober habits and had never been seen the worse of drink.

Henry's other evidence went much the same way, and Charles Gilbert Duncan applied to the Sheriff for a warrant for Henry's arrest on a charge of "culpable neglect in the discharge of his duty as Inspector of Poor". This was granted, but needless to say the Town Clerk was not actually incarcerated: he remained free while Duncan collected more evidence and referred the case for the opinion of the Crown Office in Edinburgh. Henry engaged an Edinburgh solicitor and carried on as usual until late April, when he resigned his office as Inspector of Poor without explanation. The Chief Archivist thinks his solicitor may have warned him that his case was poor, and that resigning was his best hope of avoiding proceedings. The Crown Office, after months of dithering, recommended no further action.

The family Kirstie had fought so hard to keep together was split up. James, being sixteen, had no claim on the Board and found lodgings, probably as a farm servant (much the kind of life his parents had hoped to spare him.) Johnie was adopted by a man living in a rural hamlet near Lerwick. The two boys do not seem to appear in later records and may have emigrated.

Peerie Kirstie, when 18, went to Scotland and found work as an attendant in various insane asylums. In her twenties she became depressed and suicidal, unable to eat or sleep properly, (she was treating the insomnia with a mixture of chloral, brandy and laudanum) and was for a while admitted as a patient to an asylum where she had worked. She came off the drugs, was discharged as a patient and taken on again as an attendant (one wonders how interchangeable these categories were). But the depression had left her sunk in a deep apathy; she lost the job and left: destination unknown.

Charles Gilbert Duncan, apart from being Procurator Fiscal, was at one time or another chief magistrate, town councillor, agent for the Commercial Bank and consul for Belgium and Holland. In the 1860s and 70s he introduced road improvements, a more effective police system, and, most crucially, Lerwick's first piped water and sewage scheme, in the face of bitter opposition from the wealthier ratepayers who thought more of the costs than the benefits. (One way he persuaded them was by doing the legal work in connection with the scheme, free of charge.) He was knighted by the Dutch and Belgian governments for his consular work, and died in 1884, aged sixty-eight, still a single man.

BIBLIOGRAPHY

I have made use of the following books:

Lerwick: The Birth and Growth of an Island Town, by James W. Irvine, pub. Lerwick Community Council, 1985.

Traditional Life in Shetland, by James R. Nicolson, pub. Robert Hale, 1978.

Travellers in a bygone Shetland, an anthology, by Derek Flinn, pub. Scottish Academic Press, 1989.

A Lerwick Miscellany, by E. S. Reid Tait.

The State of the Scottish Working Class in 1843, by Levitt & Smout, pub. Scottish Academic Press, 1979.